SECOND CHANCE WITH THE BILLIONAIRE

A SWEET HOLIDAY CONTEMPORARY ROMANCE

ANNE-MARIE MEYER

To my sister
You found your own Mr. Blake

CHAPTER ONE

HANNAH

Hannah stood outside of the front door of her childhood home, trying to stay dry. It was pouring rain in North Carolina—something she would have remembered had this not been the first time she'd come home in over seven years.

She sighed as she pushed a wet curl from her face. Of course she didn't have an umbrella. In her hasty plan to run away from Samson, she'd forgotten that Christmastime was rainy season. But when a man you're not ready to marry asks you—you have no choice but to high-tail it out of there.

Hannah shuffled farther under the stoop. The wreath her mom had picked was insane. It hung on the front door like a giant beacon, screaming to anyone who drove by that the woman who lived here was trying to compensate for something.

Just knock and get out of the rain, she chanted in her mind.

She tried to shove the wreath to one side. It wouldn't budge. She tried to move it to the other side. Still wouldn't budge. The green foliage had been trapped between the closed door and the frame. Bending down, she knocked on the few inches of door she could locate. Nothing.

A car honked.

Heat crept up across her skin. She didn't want to be here, and now she was fighting with a Christmas decoration to get inside. She whipped around and waved at the taxi driver who had backed out of the driveway.

The short, balding man pointed to the spot in front of his car door.

Sighing, Hannah abandoned her luggage, lifted her purse over her head, and raced over to him as water soaked her feet.

"You can go," she said before his window was halfway down.

He smacked his gum between his lips and shook his head. "Sorry, sweetie. Rules state that if I leave you in front of a house, you gotta sign a waiver. You know, in case you die from hypothermia." He shoved a clipboard toward her.

"Really?"

He winked at her. "Can't have people suing me."

"But I'd be dead," she mumbled as she unclipped the pen from the board, scribbled her name at the bottom, and handed it back.

"Perfect. Thanks! Here's my card. Call me if no one answers." He flung the business card through the window and sped off.

She squatted down and fished it out before it sank to its watery death. Then she raced back to the stoop. Shaking off the droplets, she tucked it into the back pocket of her jeans.

This was just great. Pulling her coat tighter against her body, she glanced around. The standard front light was on, but that meant nothing. Ever since Mom and Dad divorced, Mom always kept that light on. She told Hannah it was to ward off intruders. Hannah peered down the street. This was a small town. What would happen here?

She picked up her purse and opened it. After a few seconds, she pulled out her phone. After turning it on, she scrolled through her contacts until she found *Mom*.

"Beep."

Ring.

Hannah sighed. The inside phone was ringing.

"Beep."

Ring.

Pulling the phone from her face, she groaned. Technically challenged Mom refused to get a cell phone. Hopelessness filled her chest. She was out of options. The taxi driver predicted it. This was how she was going to die. In nowhere North Carolina with a tacky wreath as her only companion. She should have known better than to come home. What was she thinking?

A thundering noise broke her reverie. Glancing next door, she saw a dark figure race up the driveway, pulling a trash can behind them. The Blake residence. Anger filled her stomach as she turned back to the door. Nope. She would never. Nothing would make her that desperate to go over there again. Not after what Logan did to her.

She pounded on the door. The sound was muffled by the layers of holiday cheer. Mom had to be here. She had to.

But there was no answer.

Lifting her phone up, she punched in her dad's number.

"Hannah?"

She sighed. Salvation. "Hi, Dad."

"Hey, honey. How was your flight?"

"Eh, uneventful. Hey, are you home? I'm at Mom's, and she's not here."

There was silence. "She's not?"

"No. I caught an earlier flight, and I'm now standing outside in the rain."

"Hannah, sweetie, I would love to help you, but I'm not home right now. Actually, I'm three hours away."

Ugh. Hannah's shoulders dropped. "Seriously?"

"And, besides, you know how strict your mom is about her time with you."

Apparently, it wasn't that important for her to not show up at the airport and to not be home. Did she not even check her messages now? She said she had the day off. "Yeah, you're right."

"Go over to the Blakes' and wait."

Hannah shook her head. *Nope.* "Good idea, Dad. Thanks!"

"Love you, honey. I'll see you Christmas Day."

"Love you, too."

Hannah shoved her phone back into her purse. Typical. Neither of her parents were around, and she was left alone, again.

"Hannah?"

"Agh!" She whipped around. A woman hidden by an umbrella stood behind her.

"Ted thought that was you. What're you doing, honey?"

"Mrs. Blake?" Hannah peered down to the silver-haired woman who was peeking at her from under the polka dot material.

"Of course, sweetie. Your mom's not going to be home for a few more hours. She picked up another shift at the hospital."

Hannah pushed her water-drenched hair from her face. "Of course."

"You're welcome to come over and wait."

Hannah peered over to the two-story house that had once been her home away from home. Her stomach knotted. "Are you sure that's okay? I don't want to intrude."

Mrs. Blake reached down and grabbed one of her bags. "No more questions. Of course, it's okay. I just pulled out some bread from the oven and can't eat it all myself."

A rumble erupted in Hannah's stomach. That did sound enticing. The only thing she had eaten all day was a bag of over-priced, stale peanuts.

She eyed the cream-colored house. Going back there meant facing her past and that was the last thing she wanted to do today.

Before she could come up with an excuse, Mrs. Blake turned and walked back to her house with Hannah's bag still clutched in her hand. "Come on," she called over her shoulder.

Hannah sighed and tucked her suitcase further under the stoop. She raised her purse over her head and started after her. This encounter was inevitable—might as well get it over with.

The warmth enveloped Hannah as she stomped her feet on the mat and shut the door. The smell of homemade bread and cinnamon filled her senses. The feeling of Christmastime had a magical effect on her nerves, and she felt the tension that had built up in her muscles disappear.

"Mrs. Blake, it smells amazing," she said as she slipped off her coat and hung it in the closet. A perfectly decorated Christmas tree twinkled in the corner of the living room. Christmas decorations were something Mrs. Blake was famous for.

"Thank you, sweetie," she called from the kitchen.

Hannah pulled off her shoes and winced as she realized that her socks were soaked. Thankfully, the piece of luggage Mrs. Blake grabbed was the one with all her underwear and socks. Unzipping the bag, she rifled through it and emerged with a pair of dry socks. Once her toes were warm, she shoved the wet ones into her coat pocket.

"What're you doing?"

Hannah yelped. Standing behind her was a young girl, no older than seven. Her forehead was wrinkled. "What're you doing?" she repeated.

Hannah's cheeks heated, but she forced herself to smile. "My socks were wet."

"Huh. Do you normally bring a change of socks everywhere you go? And"—the girl stepped forward and peered into the bag—"underwear?"

Hannah reached out and pulled it from view. "I'm actually—"

"Are you coming?" Mrs. Blake appeared in the hall. "Oh, I see you've met Piper."

Piper pulled at one of the red curls that hung just below her shoulder. "Grandma, did you know she brings underwe—"

"Yes, we met." Hannah stepped in front of the bag and smiled.

Mrs. Blake nodded. "Well, come into the kitchen. Bread's been cut."

Grateful for a distraction, Hannah entered the kitchen. Mrs. Blake handed her a plate with a piece of bread that was still steaming.

"Honey's on the counter."

After drizzling her bread, Hannah made her way over to the table and sat. So many memories of sitting with Logan, studying, laughing, watching movies flooded her mind. Frustrated with herself, she began to shove the bread into her mouth in an attempt to stifle her thoughts.

"Goodness, you were hungry," Mrs. Blake said as she slid another slice of bread onto Hannah's plate.

Hannah smiled and chewed. After Mrs. Blake set two mugs on the table, she sat down next to her.

"So, you're home for the holidays," she said as she sipped at the steaming tea.

Hannah nodded, lifting her mug to her lips and tipping it. Scalding hot liquid coated her throat, and she winced. Her tongue was raw as she rubbed it against the roof of her mouth. Her eyes watered as she forced a grin toward Mrs. Blake.

"Sorry, hon. It's hot. I should've warned you."

"It's okay," Hannah managed out.

"How long are you going to be here? I have to say, your mom's so excited to have you home. It's been what? Seven years?"

Hannah nodded again.

"You probably saw the wreath." Mrs. Blake leaned over. "I helped her pick it out. She wanted this holiday to be special for you."

A snort escaped. Hannah's hand flew to her mouth. "I'm sorry."

Mrs. Blake studied her, then reached out and covered Hannah's hand with hers. "It's okay. I understand. You guys have a rocky past. You know, there isn't a day that goes by that your mom doesn't regret what happened."

Tears stung her eyes as Hannah glanced down at the oak table in front of her. Her throat tightened. She knew these memories were going to come up, and she thought she was prepared for it. What a joke.

The back door slammed, followed by a deep voice. "Ma?"

Hannah's heart sank.

"Logan, we're in here."

Hannah pulled her hand from Mrs. Blake and glanced around, wishing she could disappear. Or crawl under the table. Would they notice that?

"We?" he called from the mudroom.

Her heart pounded from the familiar cadence of his voice.

"Hannah Bell's here."

Silence.

"She's visiting her mom, but her mom wasn't there, so I invited her over."

More silence.

"You still there?" Mrs. Blake called.

Logan's six-foot frame filled the doorway. Hannah felt the gaze of his pale blue eyes fall on her as he entered. "Yeah, of course I'm here, Ma." He shot Mrs. Blake an annoyed look, then ran his hand through his dark brown hair, causing water droplets to fly through the air. "Hey, Hannah. Haven't seen you in a long time."

The lump in her throat had grown three times since he entered. She wanted to say something, but feared the sound her voice would make, so she nodded.

Mrs. Blake glanced at Hannah and then back to Logan. "Well, this is nice. I haven't seen you two together since, what? Prom?"

"Ma!" Logan whipped around and glared at her.

Hannah stood, slamming her knee against the bottom of the table. She winced, but held it together. "I should go."

Mrs. Blake sat there with her mouth open. "Was it something I said?"

"Ma, will you drop it?" Logan walked farther into the room.

Hannah wanted to run. For the first time in her life she was grateful that she had spent so many years doing track. She was sure she could outrun the both of them. Well, at least Mrs. Blake and her insistent need to relive painful memories. "Thank you for the food and the shelter, but I should be going." She turned and headed toward the front door. It felt as if the walls were closing in on her.

"Hannah, where will you go?" Mrs. Blake called after her.

"Hannah!" Logan was two steps behind her.

"It's okay. I'll be okay. I'll just go to town and get the keys from my mom. I'm so stupid. Why didn't I think of that before?" She grabbed her purse and blinked, willing the tears to retreat.

"Listen, I'll go. You stay." Logan was inches from her.

"No. Don't be ridiculous. This is your house. I'll go." She reached out and grabbed for her suitcase. Underwear and socks tumbled to the ground. Heat raged on her cheeks as she cursed fate's sense of humor. "I'm sorry," she stammered as she knelt down and started to shove her personal items back into the bag.

"Let me help." Logan was next to her, picking up her bras and handing them over.

Mortified, Hannah kept her gaze on the task at hand. "Thanks," she said, grabbing them from his outstretched hand. Inside, she was willing herself back to her apartment in Ohio. Away from this place. Away from these memories.

Making sure the suitcase was shut this time, Hannah grabbed the handles and stood. Logan was still next to her. She could feel his stare. She reached for the door handle and turned it.

"It's good to see you," Logan said. His voice was low, and his breath smelled of mint.

She nodded, not meeting his gaze, then slipped out into the pouring rain. As the water ran down her face, she let her tears flow. At least out here, no one would notice.

CHAPTER TWO

LOGAN

Logan stood by the front door, staring at it. His stomach was in knots as he tried to analyze what had just happened. Hannah was here. In his parent's house. And she'd talked to him. That was more than he'd ever gotten her to do since prom.

"You okay, honey?" his mom asked from behind him.

He nodded. But deep down, it was a lie.

A warm hand rested on his arm. He glanced over to see the furrowed brow of his mom. "You sure?"

"Yeah. It was just strange, you know?"

She smiled. "I'm happy it happened. It's about time you kids started talking again. You were always so close. It's time she learned the truth." She dropped her hand and started to make her way back to the kitchen. "Coming?"

Logan took one last look at the door and turned. Just as he passed the stairs, he noticed a piece of lacy black fabric. He reached down and picked it up. His cheeks burned. It was Hannah's underwear.

"I have some..." his mom started to say as she appeared in the kitchen door frame. Her mouth hung open as she eyed him.

Suddenly, he became very aware of how visible the underwear was. He glanced over at her. "I—this—It's Hannah's," he stammered as he crumpled up the underwear and shoved it into his front pocket.

His mom's eyebrows rose.

"I should bring it back to her."

She nodded. "But first, tell me how the meeting went."

Logan glanced at the door, and then back to his mom. He contemplated racing to it, but stopped himself. His mom was only going to keep asking. Besides, if he were honest with himself, he felt like he needed a moment to compose his emotions before he saw Hannah again.

He headed toward the kitchen, still not believing everything was finalized. It had been months of meeting with his dad's lawyer and today was the last session. Everything that his father had owned was now his. He was a billionaire.

Three years ago, his dad came into his life after being MIA since Logan was born. He'd recently found out that he had cancer and wanted to make amends before he passed. For Logan, knowing his real dad had always been something he'd wanted. A year ago, his dad sold his multi-billion-dollar tech company and set up a trust for him.

"Well," Logan said as he moved to lean against the kitchen counter. "It's done."

It had been an emotional year since his dad passed. Even though his bank account now had more zeros than he could have ever imagined, he was finding it hard to use any of it. He missed his dad too much. It felt wrong to spend it.

His mom settled in next to the table and sipped her tea. "That's great, honey. Any idea what you're going to do now?"

She picked chunks of bread off and slipped them into her mouth.

Logan pinched his lips. What was she thinking? This was a small town. News like this would travel fast. He loved his mom, but she wasn't discreet.

"Mom," Logan groaned. He could see the wheels spinning in her gaze as she studied him.

She shrugged. "This is a small town, Logan. That money could go to help a lot of people."

Anger pricked at the back of his neck. He didn't like where this conversation was going. Was this his fate? Once everyone in town found out his net worth, could he trust their intentions?

He clenched his jaw and shoved his hands into his pockets. After taking a deep breath, he let it out slowly. This was not what he wanted to think about right now. His fingers brushed the lace of Hannah's underwear. Tension left his shoulders. He had an excuse to leave.

"I'm gonna head over and return Hannah's things to her," Logan said as he all but sprinted toward the back door.

His mom's face fell, but she nodded. "I still think we should tal—"

"Yep," he interjected. "Watch Piper for me?"

His mom waved her hand and picked up a magazine that was stacked on the far end of the table.

Once outside, he took a deep breath. He didn't mind the rain that drizzled from the sky. It seemed to ground him. He ducked his head and headed over to Hannah's house. He couldn't focus on his conversation with his mom anymore. Right now, there was a girl standing on her stoop next door with bright green eyes that made his heart race. He needed to steel his nerves for the upcoming interaction. Especially when he had no idea what he was going to say.

HANNAH

"Bert McMillan," the familiar southern accent shouted through the phone. Then he paused. "She's not home, is she?"

Hannah gritted her teeth as she slunk farther under the stoop. She had her phone pressed to her ear and was gripping the taxi driver's business card in the other. "How'd you—?"

"Eh, girl, when you've been a taxi driver as long as I have, you get a sense of situations. Girl finally comes home after a long period of time. Parents forgot. Probably a broken relationship with a boy mixed in."

She pulled the phone from her cheek as her lips parted. She stared down at the screen. Who was this guy? Clearing her throat, she raised it back up to her ear. "Well, I'm hoping since you are an all-knowing taxi driver, you didn't go far. Can you pick me up and give me a ride to the hospital?"

He paused. "Hospital? But you signed the wavier."

"I'm not going because of that. I need a ride to my mom. She'll have the key."

The smacking of his gum filled the air once more. "No can do, sweetie. My cab waits for no girl. I have a drop-off to make right now, but I'll swing by after. Anything for my most loyal customer."

"How long?" Hannah growled as she glanced out at the torrential rain. Thankfully, she had composed herself enough to make this call. All she wanted to do right now was take a hot shower and curl up with a good book on her childhood bed that was probably still covered with a bit too many stuffed animals.

"Eh, thirty minutes?"

She sighed. "Fine. See you in thirty." She punched the end call button and dropped her phone into her purse. Turning her suitcase to its side, she shoved it against the house and sunk down onto it. Wind nipped at her arms, so she pulled her jacket closer. It was hard to believe that the ocean was only a few miles off.

Her gaze wandered back over to the Blakes' residence and the last twenty minutes replayed in her mind. Mrs. Blake. Logan. The familiar house and feelings. They all came rushing back to her. Why did Mrs. Blake have to bring up prom like she did? Hannah had spent so long trying to forget that dreadful night. One mention of it and all of Hannah's hard work was thrown out the window.

Reaching up, she touched her lips. They still tingled from the memory. The song, *When a Man loves a Woman,* blared through the speakers. Logan's arm wrapped around her waist. They stopped dancing. He reached out his hand and cradled her cheek. Suddenly, he leaned forward, causing her heart to pound in her chest.

Hannah closed her eyes. Why did it always have to feel so real? It was seven years ago; surely something would have faded by now.

"Hannah?"

See, even his voice was as clear as the night he'd kissed her.

"Hannah."

Why couldn't this memory just leave her alone?

A hand grabbed her elbow. "Hannah!"

This wasn't a memory. Whipping her eyes open, a groan erupted in her throat. Logan's quizzical eyes were staring back at her.

"You okay?" he asked.

She pushed herself forward and stood. He was inches from her. The stoop was barely big enough for the two of them. "Yep, uh-huh." Mentally, she slapped herself. Why did she have to sound like such an idiot? Not sure what to do, she wrapped her arms around her chest and glanced over at him. "So, what's up?"

"Um, well..." He paused as his cheeks turned red. "You left this." Reaching his hand out, he uncurled his fingers to reveal a pair of her lace panties.

Mortified, she grabbed them. "Oh, my gosh," she sputtered as she shoved the underwear into her coat pocket, wishing that a hole would open up and swallow her.

Logan tucked his hands into the front pockets of his jeans and glanced around. "Mom's not home, huh?"

She swallowed hard, trying to push every emotion down that she could. "Yeah, looks that way."

He glanced up and down the street. "Cab coming?"

"Excuse me?" Her mind was muddled.

"When you ran out, you mentioned something about going to town. I figured you'd call a cab."

His words began to make sense. She nodded. "He's coming. This is the last time I don't rent a car."

He nodded. "Mind if I wait with you? I'd love to catch up."

Hannah's heart pounded. She hoped he couldn't hear it. "Oh, no. That's okay. I'm sure you have better things to do. Besides, he'll be here in like twenty minutes. I'd hate to inconvenience you."

"Twenty minutes?"

Hannah pinched her lips together. Had she just said that? "I'm sure it's not going to take that long."

Logan reached out and grabbed all of her luggage. "Enough said. I'm giving you a ride." He turned and retreated back to his house with her things.

Grumbling, Hannah shoved her hands in her coat pockets and left the steps for the second time today. What was it with the Blake family and stealing people's suitcases? Hannah had half a mind to just let him take her luggage and stay on the steps. After all, it was one less thing for her to worry about.

As her fingers brushed her underwear and wet socks, she sighed. She couldn't leave her stuff with him. What if all the clasps decided not to work and the suitcases burst open? Knowing her luck, that would happen.

She grabbed her phone and hit talk. It dialed the most recent number.

"I'm coming, girlie. It's gonna take me a bit," Bert said.

"Scratch that. I seemed to suddenly have a ride."

His laugh filled the air. "The boy who broke your heart?"

Hannah stammered. "Ye-yeah."

His laugh trickled down to a low rumble. "Keep my phone number on hand for the future. I'd like to see how this goes for you." He paused. "In fact, I'll give you a 50 percent discount."

That was strange. "To drive me around?"

"Yep."

"I'll hold you to that."

He laughed. "I don't doubt it."

Hannah pulled the phone from her ear and hit end.

She glanced in the direction Logan had gone and sighed. With no ride coming, she was going to have to brave the twenty-minute drive in his presence. But the problem with that was, she was letting him back into her life. And that was something she'd promised herself, years ago, she would never do.

CHAPTER THREE

HANNAH

Logan was shoving all her luggage into the back of his pickup when she rounded the house. After slamming the tailgate closed, he rushed over to the passenger door and rested his hand on the handle. "I was afraid you wouldn't come."

Hannah managed a smile. "Well, you took my luggage, so I really didn't have a choice."

His smile faltered but remained. She neared him, and he pulled open the door.

"You really didn't have to," she said as she placed her foot on the step and went to grab the chair and handle. Suddenly, a warm hand engulfed hers. Startled, she turned to see Logan glance at her and then down to the ground. She wanted to drop his hand, but the familiar emotions that rushed from her fingers to her heart paralyzed her.

"Listen, Hannah. I know what you think of me. What I did was... well, it was inexcusable. If only you knew—"

"Logan, please. Let's just get to the hospital. It's been years, and I've moved on. I'm sure you have as well." She dropped his hand and shifted in the seat to reach for the seatbelt.

Logan stood in the rain, staring off into the distance. Water dripped from his hair and rolled down his face. As much as Hannah wanted to deny it, he looked amazing.

She pulled her gaze from his face and studied the shut garage door in front of her. She cursed the woodsy smell of his cologne that threatened to activate the tears she was forcing down.

"You're right," he said as he slammed the door and raced around to the driver's side.

He got in and turned the key. The truck roared to life, and he backed it down the driveway. They rode in silence for a few minutes. Hannah's cheeks burned with every glance he shot her way.

"So, how's life after college been?" he asked.

"Great. I love my job. I'm looking at getting my master's, but it costs money."

"Yeah? What would you get your master's in?" He kept his attention on the road.

"Social work."

"You'd be good at that," Logan said as he shot her a half-smile.

Hannah nodded and silence engulfed the car once more.

"So, did you meet a lot of guys in Ohio?" His question came out barely a whisper.

Hannah paused. She wasn't sure what to say. Should she tell him about Samson? She wasn't even sure how she felt about him or his proposal. Plus, it felt strange replaying the situation to Logan. But she couldn't say nothing at all. "Eh, too many to count."

Logan's gaze fell on her, and his jaw flexed. "That's nice," he finally said.

Hannah shifted in her seat. This ride was getting more and more uncomfortable. "So, you? How's life been going for you?"

He flicked on his blinker and changed lanes. "Ah, well, I finally met my dad."

Hannah stared at the water droplets that rolled horizontally across her window. "Really? How'd that happen?"

That was something he'd always wanted. It wasn't that his stepdad was bad. But there had always been a hole in his heart from the absence of his real dad.

"He came around about three years ago. He had terminal cancer."

Hannah's heart sank. What did Logan mean *had*? "Is he—I mean, has he passed on?"

Logan nodded, and Hannah's stomach sank. "I'm so sorry," she said, wishing there was something more she could say.

Logan took a deep breath. "Yeah. It's been an emotional few years."

Hannah nodded. That was true for the both of them. There were moments she'd wished she could have called him up just to hear his voice. But it never felt right.

"It was nice to see your mom." Hannah thought it was best to move the conversation forward. After all, that's what she wanted when people brought up difficult subjects. "She's always been an amazing cook. Remember when she made that five-tier cake, and we accidentally left it out? And Tumor got it?" She smiled at the thought of the neighbor's bulldog tearing through the neighborhood, covered in icing. He was trying to get away from Mrs. Blake who was red-faced and swearing.

Logan let out a deep laugh. A sound Hannah was all too familiar with. It made her heart soar that she'd brought him some happiness.

"That was an epic day." He shot her a smile that lit up his entire face.

The laughter died down to silence. It felt good to laugh with him once more. It had been so long since she'd seen him. The day after prom, she'd packed up and left, unable to talk to him or Mom again. Her mom was devastated that she moved to her dad's, but what other choice did she have? She couldn't live in that house anymore.

Hannah's smile faded as she turned her attention back outside. The large "H" sign with an arrow underneath signaled that they were minutes away. She reached down and grabbed her purse. "You can just drop me off at the front."

"But your luggage—"

"I'll be fine. I got it all the way here on my own."

Logan pursed his lips, but then nodded. "Okay."

He pulled the truck up to the front entrance and threw it into park. Opening his door, he jumped out and raced around to the other side before Hannah could open her door. Not waiting for his hand, she leapt down and slung her purse over her shoulder. "Thanks for giving me a ride. You saved me a half-hour of waiting in the rain."

He nodded, then walked around to the tailgate and pulled it open. He unloaded her suitcases. "Of course. Anytime, Hanny B."

Her face flushed at the familiar nickname that only Logan was allowed to call her. She met his gaze and, in that moment, all pain that she had felt for so long dulled.

His lips rose into a half-smile as he pushed his hand through his hair. "Sorry. I should've probably asked if that nickname was still okay."

Hannah swallowed. "Of course, you can always call me that." Her throat tightened, making her voice come out hoarse. She chewed her lip and cursed the emotions that exposed her.

"You sure you don't want me to help you wheel in your luggage?" He nodded toward the three bags he had unloaded.

"You don't want them dumping out in there." He eyed the bag that had spilled earlier.

Heat radiated from her cheeks. She shook her head. "No, I'll be okay. They all kind of clip together."

He slammed the tailgate closed and glanced at her. The look in his eyes told her he wanted to say more, but wasn't sure how.

She wasn't sure she wanted to know. "I'll be okay. Thanks for the ride again." Not knowing what to do, she reached out her hand.

Logan glanced at it and then back up to her. "Anytime you need a ride, I'm happy to help." He grabbed her hand and shook it a few times. He kept his gaze locked with hers.

"I'll remember that." The desire to give her a ride seemed to be a common theme today. She pulled away from him and grabbed the handles of her luggage, trying to ignore the memory of his skin against hers.

She walked toward the hospital doors that opened as she approached. Once inside, she turned to see him throw his keys into the air and walk over to the driver's door and climb in. A few seconds later, he peeled away.

Hannah slumped against the wall. What was she doing to herself?

LOGAN

Logan tried to keep his focus on the road as he drove away from the hospital. The memory of Hannah's hand heated his skin. He leaned over and cranked up the air. Even though it was December, he needed to cool down.

He twisted his hand around the steering wheel. Why couldn't he just tell her what had happened? He'd tried, but she wouldn't let him. He pushed his free hand through his hair.

She needed to know why he walked out that night. Even if it didn't change how she felt about him, she still needed to know.

The rain stopped, allowing the sun to push through the clouds. Logan reached over and grabbed his sunglasses. By the time he pulled into his driveway, the ground was dry.

Jumping down from his truck, he slammed the door.

"Hey, Daddy," a sweet voice called to him.

Smiling, Logan turned around. "Hey, Pip."

His seven-year-old daughter grinned back at him. Her curly red hair stuck out from under her bike helmet. She rode up to him and stopped. "Where'd you go?"

Logan tucked his keys into his pocket. "I was giving a friend a ride into town."

She crinkled her nose. "The lady who brings her underwear around with her?"

Heat flushed his cheeks at the memory of holding Hannah's personal items. "Yes. That lady."

Piper played with the bell on the handle of her bike. "She was weird."

"Piper." He gave her a pointed look.

She shrugged. "What? It's weird to bring that stuff around with you."

"She's visiting her mom, Miss Kathy, that's why she had all that stuff with her. It's her luggage."

Piper chewed her lip. "Oh." Then she twisted her handle, causing the tire to scrape the road. "Has my mom called yet?"

Logan's heart plummeted at the mention of his ex-wife. Charity wasn't reliable at all. She was supposed to take Piper for the holiday, but yet again, she flaked out. It seemed that now, her new method of disappointing their daughter was to never return Piper's phone calls. That was followed by never showing up and never following through with promises.

"I'm not sure, sweetie. I had an important meeting earlier

this morning and had my phone turned off. Maybe she called and I missed it."

Piper kept her gaze fixed on the driveway. "Yeah. Probably."

He pulled out his phone, willing there to be a message from Charity. Nothing. Zip. She'd abandoned her daughter once again. Shoving the phone into his back pocket, he walked over and pulled Piper into a hug. "It's going to be okay. She'll call." He hated lying to her, but he didn't know what else to do.

She nodded against his shoulder. "Bike to the beach with me?"

Logan smiled. "Of course."

She grinned and pulled away from him. "Hurry up."

He raced over to the garage door and pulled it open. Grabbing his bike, he wheeled it over to where Piper was biking up and down the street. He unhooked his helmet and snapped it under his chin.

Soon, he was pedaling next to her. She giggled like she was holding onto a secret.

"Race you!" she screamed and took off.

"Hey! That's not fair," he called after her, but a smile played on his lips. It was just like his daughter to do something like that.

Five minutes down and they stopped right before the sand. Water lapped at the shore as they dismounted and pushed the kickstands down. They left their shoes by their bikes. Sand squished between Logan's toes as he raced after her. She was headed for the water. They allowed the waves to race over their feet, but that was as far as they would go. Water temperature plummeted this time of year.

After scouring the beach for shark teeth and shells, Logan settled down on the sand and watched his daughter poke at some washed-up seaweed with a stick.

His heart ached at what his ex did to their daughter. She loved her mother, and the fact that Charity couldn't care less angered him. There was nothing and no one that would keep him from his little girl. If only his ex had that same kind of commitment.

His thoughts returned to the conversation with his mom. His dad had given him permission to do what he thought was best with the money. He trusted Logan. But right now, all Logan wanted to do was pretend that it wasn't there. Just take small amounts out so he could spend time with his daughter and quit all the odd jobs he'd had to pick up in the past to survive. But that was it.

Leave it to his mom to pressure him into spending it. Logan harrumphed and pushed his toes into the sand as he studied the waves. It seemed that even though he wanted things to remain the same, his life had been forever changed.

CHAPTER FOUR

HANNAH

The sterilized smell of hospital air filled Hannah's nose as she willed her body to calm down. The coolness of the wall behind her seeped through her shirt, grounding her to earth. She had her first encounter with Logan and survived. One point for her.

"Dr. Johnson. Dr. Johnson to the ER," a nasally voice announced over the intercom. The soft Christmas music that came from the piano in the far side of the room returned to normal volume.

Hannah glanced around and took in the people who were meandering through the lobby. Some were talking in hushed voices, others had furrowed brows and tear-stained faces. Hannah's heart went out to them. Maybe that's why she'd dedicated her whole life to social work despite how her mother felt.

How could she not when she'd spent so many nights after school slumped on one of the worn-out couches, waiting for her mom to finish her rounds? All the people she'd interacted with contributed to her desire to help others. When she'd told her mom what she wanted to do, her mom grew quiet.

Apparently, years of working with teenage moms seemed to have tainted her. She told Hannah she wanted her to have nothing to do with those types of people. Anger coursed through Hannah's veins as she glanced around.

Everything exploded on prom night. The memory caused Hannah's spine to tingle. It was the night that the two most important people in her life betrayed her.

Taking in a deep breath, Hannah let it out slowly. She couldn't think about that right now. She pushed off the wall and straightened, shoving the memories deep down where they belonged. She couldn't go meet her mom for the first time in seven years emotionally charged. And she couldn't stay down in the lobby forever.

She made her way to the elevator with the tips of her fingers curled around the luggage handles. Reaching out, she slapped the up button and waited, keeping an eye trained on the elevator lights.

"Hannah Banana?"

Ugh, that nickname should have died years ago.

"Hannah?"

Taking a deep breath, she turned.

Bright green eyes behind dark-rimmed glasses gazed back at her.

"Sandy?" she sputtered.

A wide smile, sans braces, spread across her high school best friend's face. "It's been so long! I can't believe you're here!" Sandy opened her arms and pulled Hannah into a giant hug.

Unsure of what to do, Hannah patted her back. After a moment, Sandy pulled away.

"How have you been?" Sandy asked as she pulled her purse

strap back onto her shoulder and took a step back. "I haven't seen you in forever."

"Oh, I've been good. You know. Work keeps me busy."

"That's right. You were always a book-smart girl." Sandy reached out and play-punched Hannah's shoulder. "And Ohio? That's awesome. It's good you got away." She moved closer to accommodate the crowd of doctors and nurses who were gathering by the elevators.

"Yep." Hannah nodded. In a small town like Beaufort, it was hard to get away.

"Here to see your mom?"

Hannah peered up at the elevator lights. If the elevator ever came. "Yep."

Sandy glanced over at her luggage. "She forgot about you, didn't she?"

Hannah grabbed the handles tighter. "Something like that."

"At least some things never change."

Heat crept up Hannah's cheeks. She wanted to change the subject. "So, are you visiting someone?"

Sandy's face brightened. "Oh my gosh, yes! My fiancé!" She reached out her hand and shoved a giant ring right under Hannah's nose. "The wedding is this weekend. The afternoon of Christmas Eve." Then her grin faltered.

Hannah peered over at her. "What's wrong?"

"It's just all a mess. My fiancé just got in an accident—"

Hannah's eyebrows shot up.

Sandy waved her hand. "Don't worry. It's nothing too serious, and thankfully, it won't show up in the pictures."

"That's rough." Hannah was grateful to hear that he was okay.

"Well, it doesn't end there. Apparently, my maid of honor has shingles and can't come. None of my bridesmaids can fly in early, so I'm stuck."

The elevator door dinged, and Hannah followed after Sandy. Soon, they were standing inches apart as doctors and nurses stepped in after them.

Hannah glanced over to Sandy who had a glint in her eyes. "What?" Hannah asked.

"I have an idea— you could be my maid of honor." Sandy moved a few inches back and ran her gaze up and down Hannah's body. "Yeah, you are about the same size as Patricia."

Hannah stared at her. What was happening? "I'm sorry. What? Who's Patricia?"

Sandy waved her hand. "Ugh. It's Jimmy's sister who was supposed to be my maid of honor, but now has shingles. Geez, girl, keep up."

"And why is it important that she and I are the same size?"

Sandy's smile faltered. "Because you're going to be my maid of honor." She gripped onto Hannah's arm. "Come on, it'll be fun. Please?"

Hannah glanced around. A few doctors were studying their interaction. Saying no felt wrong. "I guess."

Sandy threw her arms around Hannah as she squealed. "Yay! Okay, this is my floor, but I'll call you with details."

The elevator rang as it stopped on floor three. Sandy moved to slip through the open doors. "I'll call you at your mom's. Is that okay?"

Hannah nodded.

"Oh, and I should probably tell you. Logan Blake's the best man—" she yelled as the elevator doors closed on her voice.

Hannah heart sank. What did she just say? Logan? She wanted to stop the elevator and make it go back down so she could clarify what Sandy had said. Unfortunately, it just kept going up. Her shoulders slumped. There was no getting out of this.

The elevator door opened on floor six, Labor and Delivery,

and Hannah's stomach flipped. She couldn't worry about that commitment right now. She'd deal with it later. Right now, her focus should be on the upcoming interaction with her mom.

In the foyer, two nurses stood behind the desk with charts in hand, whispering to one another. A woman clutching her swollen stomach inched past Hannah with her face contorted in pain. Hannah gave her a sympathetic look as she waited for her to pass.

With her luggage trailing behind her, Hannah approached the desk.

The older nurse, who looked like she could be Hannah's grandma, glanced up at her and then down to her stomach.

Hannah sucked in her breath, hoping there was no way this woman could mistake her as pregnant.

"What can we do for you, sweetie?" Her southern drawl seeped from her coral lips.

"Well, if it isn't Hannah Bell!" the other nurse squealed as she set her chart down and bounded around the desk.

"Loretta?" The air whooshed through Hannah's lungs as she was enveloped in a hug.

The nurse pulled away. Her overly lined eyes peered up at Hannah. "It's just been so long since I've seen you."

There was no way Hannah would forget the accent and contagious smile. Loretta was her pseudo mom all those nights she waited in the lobby as a kid.

Hannah wrapped her arms around the now pudgy woman. "It's been so long," she said as she smiled. This was a reunion. This was what it felt like to be wanted.

Loretta grinned from ear to ear. "It has! I mean, I left for a while, but now I'm back. And so are you!" She paused as she glanced at the luggage in tow. "You're not..." She motioned toward Hannah's midriff.

"Oh, no. Goodness, no. I'm here to see my mom."

Loretta giggled. "Oh, I see. Let me go grab her. She's with a patient." She started down the hall, then turned and winked. "I hope you're not too old for blue popsicles. Maybe I'll peek into the freezer and see if there are any there," Loretta called over her shoulder.

Hannah smiled at her retreating frame. It was a ritual they had. Giggling on the couch as they tried to gobble up the popsicle before it melted. It helped break up the monotony of hanging around contracting women.

Loretta disappeared around the corner, and Hannah leaned against a wall. Thankfully, the other nurse went back to charting, which allowed the lobby to fill with silence. This was the first time she would see her mom since Georgia left. Hannah's stomach twisted at the thought.

She sighed. After what Georgia had done, Hannah doubted her mom was capable of forgiving her. She studied her nails and took a deep breath. She needed to prepare for the icy reunion headed her way.

A few minutes ticked by before a familiar voice called out her name.

"Hannah, why are you here?"

Hannah swallowed and turned. "Hi, Mom."

Her mother's greying hair was pulled back into a bun with wisps of curls framing her face. She had a pair of polka dot reading glass perched on the tip of her nose. Behind the lenses, her eyes narrowed.

Hannah hated the scrutiny her mom always gave her. "I took a cab from the airport, and you weren't home. It's pouring outside, but without a key I couldn't get in," she rushed out.

"Your flight wasn't supposed to come in until nine tonight. What happened?" Her mom folded her arms.

Hannah sighed. Of course, getting an earlier flight would

be her fault. "Sorry, Mom. I tried calling you, but no one answered." She lowered her voice. "If you had a cell phone…"

"You know I don't believe in those things. Just another way to stay tied to everyone around you." Her mom's arms fell to her side as she patted her pager. "All I need is right here."

"Right, Mom. Of course." The hospital and this job were all her mom had ever needed. Why did Hannah think things had changed? She paused. "So, can I get the key? I'm guessing you're going to be here a while."

Her mom shoved her hand in her pocket and pulled out her keys. After threading the house key off, she handed it over. "I won't be home until seven. There should be food in the kitchen. Help yourself to whatever."

Hannah dropped the key into her coat pocket, right alongside her underwear and socks. "Sounds good. I'll see you when you get home."

Her mom's face relaxed as she studied Hannah. It didn't sit right with her, so she shifted her weight from foot to foot. An arm reached out, and Hannah almost smacked it away. Thankfully, she'd fought the urge. It wouldn't have gone over well. Her mom pulled her closer and held her for a moment. It was awkward, but it was a hug.

"I'm happy you're here, Hannah. It's been too many Christmases."

Hannah patted her mom's back. "Yeah, I'm happy to be here, too." Her stomach knotted at the lie. Even though she didn't know where she wanted to be or belonged, she did know this wasn't the place.

CHAPTER FIVE

LOGAN

Laughter filled the air as Logan walked into his parents' house after Piper. He furrowed his brow as he glanced in the direction of the kitchen. The thought that Hannah might be here raced through his mind, but he pushed it out. It wasn't her. There was no way she'd come back after the way she'd left before.

Piper took off her shoes and bounded up the stairs. "I'm gonna go watch a show," she said as her voice grew quiet the further she got.

"Okay," Logan called after her.

Suspicious of what was happening in the other room, he approached the doorway. Two women sat at the table across from his mom. They were laughing and drinking tea. He stepped into the room.

"Hey, Mom. Just wanted to let you know that me and Pip are home." He turned to leave. He didn't want to get stuck in a conversation with his mom's friends. They could talk forever.

"Wait a minute. Sit down." His mom beckoned him over.

Logan hesitated, then turned. This was never good. "Hey, I was hoping to catch the game..." He gave her a look.

She smiled as if pretending she didn't see him. "These ladies just have a question they wanted to ask you." She pushed out a chair, and the ladies across from her smiled.

Logan knew exactly what she was doing. It was exactly what he had feared. He clenched his fists and forced a smile. "Sure, Mom." He made his way over to the chair and sat down. He turned his attention to the women across from him.

"This is Josie and Betty. They're my friends from book club."

The woman with short grey hair smiled while the other woman with long white hair nodded. Logan felt a bit guilty for the way he was acting. They were victims of his mom's schemes. This wasn't their fault.

Logan leaned forward and grasped his hands and rested them on the tabletop. "Listen, ladies, I'm not sure what my mom said." He glared over at his mom. "But I'm really not looking for new business ventures right now."

Betty giggled, her nerves apparent in the way her gaze flitted across the room. "We understand, but..." She glanced over to Josie.

"We thought we'd pitch our idea, and then you can decide for yourself," Josie finished. "You know, for the future."

"I'm sure Logan would love to listen to whatever you have to say." Logan's mom gave him a pointed look.

He wanted to fight back. He hated the corner his mom had pushed him into. How could she? His dad's money was a sensitive subject, and she was ignoring how this made him feel.

Josie gave him a big smile. "We'd really appreciate it."

Logan sighed and nodded. "Go ahead."

Betty reached toward the ground. When she straightened,

she placed a crochet blob on the table. After stretching the ends a few times, she smoothed it down. Logan studied it. It looked like a shirt for a preemie.

"This is the Kitty Cuddle," Betty explained.

"The...Kitty Cuddle?" Logan glanced from woman to woman.

Josie nodded. "It's made from completely organic material. It's hypoallergenic and machine washable."

"Just not the dryer," Betty piped up.

Logan studied her as he nodded. Since when did cats need things to be hypoallergenic?

"It's to keep cats warm. See?" Betty flipped open the scrapbook next to her and shoved it toward Logan. Inside were pictures of a particularly disgruntled looking tabby cat who had been shoved into a tiny Kitty Cuddle. Its hair was ruffled, and its eyes were wide.

"Wow," Logan said as he flipped a page. "That is something."

"That's Mr. Sprinkles," Betty said, beaming.

"Mr."—Logan paused—"Sprinkles." He flipped another page. "He doesn't look too happy right here, huh?" He lifted up the picture where Mr. Sprinkles was half hissing, half meowing.

Betty nodded. "He was hungry."

"Anyways, we were thinking we'd charge twenty-five dollars a shirt as they take us about five hours to make," Josie said.

Logan coughed. "Twenty-five?"

Both women nodded.

"Huh." How was he going to let these women down without hurting their feelings? "Do you have a business plan? Or a pamphlet I can take?"

Betty looked at Josie. "Business plan?"

Whew, an out. "Yeah. I'm not really going to be able to make an educated decision without it. Why don't you come up with one and get it to me?"

Josie pulled out a notebook from her purse. "Business plan," she repeated as she wrote the words on the paper.

"Yeah. If you could get it to me, that would be great." He shut the scrapbook and slid it across the table.

Betty grabbed it and slipped it into her bag along with the Kitty Cuddle.

"We're going to head to the library tomorrow and figure out how to write a..." she glanced over at Josie.

"Business plan," Josie repeated.

Logan smiled and stood. "Great. Well, ladies. It was good to meet you. I look forward to that plan." He reached out and shook each woman's hand. They stood and smiled at him.

"Your mom was right. You are such a sweet boy," Josie said, patting his hand.

Logan's stomach churned. And he was going to be mean to them. He clenched his jaw. He couldn't let this money turn him into a jerk. He'd make that commitment right now. He wasn't going to change. He gave Josie's hand a quick shake. "I'm happy to help."

Betty smiled. "Until next time." Both women turned and headed out of the kitchen with Logan's mom hot on their heels.

Logan made his way over to the sink and filled up a glass of water. The women's laughter carried from the hall. He heard the door shut and the house grew quiet. His mom appeared in the doorway.

He stared at her. "Mom..."

She held up her hands. "I know. I know. I couldn't help it, Logan. They're my good friends."

"I told you I wasn't ready for this kind of thing. I'm not ready for people to know I have money." He downed his glass of water and set it next to the sink. "I don't want it to change how people treat me."

His mom walked over to the sink and grabbed his dirty glass. She pulled open the dishwasher and loaded it.

"Ma, I could have done that."

She nodded. "I know that." Her smile dropped as her gaze grew heavy.

He reached out and pulled her into a hug. She buried her face in his shoulder. "What's wrong?" He hated when his mom got like this.

Her shoulders shook. "I'm just worried about you." She pulled back and dabbed her eyes. "Ever since your dad died, you've become quiet. I feel like I'm losing you and Piper."

"Ma, you're never going to lose me or Piper. She adores you."

His mom nodded as she wiped her fingers on her palms. "You say that, but there's nothing stopping you anymore. With that money, you could go anywhere. I just... want there to be something keeping you here."

Logan smiled. "And you thought that the Kitty Cuddle was the way?"

His mom laughed. "Well, it's a start, right?" She pulled back and leaned against a nearby counter.

"It's... awful."

"Hey!" His mom reached out and swatted him.

"Twenty-five bucks. Really, mom?"

She nodded. "Well, that's not their only idea."

He reached over and grabbed an apple. "I hope not." He bit into it. He studied his mom. He knew the real reason she didn't want him to go, but she'd never say it. This family never talked about it. He opened his mouth to say something, but then closed his lips. Her shoulders were already slumped. There was no reason to bring her more heartbreak.

He pulled her into a hug again. "Love you, Mom."

Another sob escaped her lips as she nodded. "Love you, too."

HANNAH

Hannah stood outside the hospital, tapping her foot. Bert said he was ten minutes out. She glanced down both sides of the road. She wanted to get away from this place as fast as possible.

"Hannah? Hannah!"

Hannah turned to see her mom walking through the sliding doors. She furrowed her brow. What was this about? "Mom?"

"I'm glad I caught you." Her mom studied her. "I'm sure this goes without saying, but I wanted to make sure it got said."

Hannah sighed. "What, Mom?"

"No...no visitors allowed in the house." Her mom dropped her voice as she stared at Hannah.

Hannah inwardly groaned. Was she serious? *Way to bring up the past, Mom.* Forcing a smile, she stared at her. "Of course. No visitors."

Her mom folded her arms. "Good. I'll see you when I get home."

"Perfect," Hannah said through gritted teeth.

Her mom turned and walked back into the hospital. Once the doors closed, Hannah let out the groan she'd been stifling. Why did she come back? Tears pricked her eyes as she studied her luggage. What her mom failed to realize was Hannah had also been hurt when Georgia broke their trust.

But, of course, her mom couldn't see past her own pain to even comprehend her daughter's hurt. And she wondered why Hannah had left. She chewed her bottom lip. Right now, Ohio with Samson and his proposal looked better than here.

A yellow cab pulled up in the roundabout. Bert smiled and waved at her. She pulled open the back door, shoved all her luggage in, and climbed in after them. "Take me home?"

"Thompson Street. On it," Bert said as she shut the door, and he peeled out.

Hannah kept her gaze outside of the car. The trees whipped past as Bert merged onto the freeway.

"Wanna talk about it?" he asked from the front.

Hannah glanced at him in the rearview mirror. "How did you do that?"

"Do what?"

"Know my situation earlier."

Bert laughed. "Honey, I'm like a bartender. Except, I get you stuck in my car for a prolonged period of time. I hear every conversation. See every situation. After a while, it becomes like a sixth sense. I can read people."

Hannah snorted. "Well, you read me perfectly."

Bert merged into another lane. "It's pretty classic, your tale."

"My tale?"

Bert nodded. "So, how did the reunion with your mom go?"

She folded her hands in her lap. That wasn't something she really wanted to talk about. "Terrible."

"Wanna tell me what happened?"

Hannah sighed. She really didn't want to relive the past.

"I get it. It's just a long ride. Sometimes it can help you feel better to talk about it." Bert shot her a smile.

"When I was a kid, I invited someone to come live with us even though my mom was skeptical. Let's just say, Mom had been right. The person was not who she said she was. She ended up..." Hannah grew quiet as the memories flooded her mind.

She had busted into the house in tears because Logan had

disappeared after their kiss. She'd searched everywhere at prom for him just to find out he'd left her there. All Hannah wanted was for her mom to hug her and tell her everything was going to be okay. Instead, the cops were at her house. Georgia had taken all of her mother's jewelry and heirlooms.

Instead of hugging Hannah and helping her feel better, Hannah spent the night getting interrogated by her mom about Georgia's whereabouts. She'd gone to bed that night with a tear-stained face and a broken heart.

"Ended up?" Bert pulled her from her memories.

"Ended up hurting my family."

Bert let out a low whistle. "That's hard."

Hannah nodded. "Yeah. Especially when I had begged my mom to let her stay."

"But you were just a kid. She had to know that."

Hannah shrugged. "For any other mom, that would be true. Not my mom, though. I still get the feeling every time she looks at me, all she sees are the things that were stolen."

"Stolen?"

"Yeah."

"Ouch," he said as he pulled up in front of her house. The sun had dipped behind the horizon, leaving orange and yellow streaks in the sky. He pushed the car into park and turned around. "Well, sounds like you and your mom have some things to work through."

Hannah pinched her lips together and nodded. "Yep."

Bert smiled. "You never know. Christmas time is a magical time. Perhaps this year, you'll be able to put the past in the past."

She fingered the door handle as she let his words sink in. "Hopefully," she whispered, but inside, doubt clouded her mind. She was willing to move forward, but she was only half the equation.

CHAPTER SIX

HANNAH

Bert waved at her as he drove away. She sighed and pulled the house key out of her pocket. Slipping it into the lock, she turned the handle. The wreath shifted against the door as she pushed past it with her luggage trailing behind her. She stepped into the foyer, set her suitcase down, and glanced around.

Not much had changed in the seven years since she'd been in this house. The same yellow couch sat parallel with the longest wall. A few decorative pillows dotted the matching armchair and love seat in the room. Besides the wreath on the door, no one would have suspected it was Christmas. There was no tree, no stockings, and no stuffed snowmen that sang and jingled.

Turning, she shut the door behind her. She had to give it an extra shove to press the wreath enough and allow the handle to engage. The ticking of the grandfather clock next to her filled the silence.

"I'm home," she muttered. The words tasted odd on her tongue. She slipped off her shoes, grabbed her suitcases, and headed to the nearby stairs.

At the top step, she paused. Her mom's room sat to the left of where she stood, and her childhood room was on the right. Across from it was the guest room—Georgia's room.

She wheeled her luggage down the hall and glanced into the open door. A lone desk sat under the window with a sleeping monitor on top of it. A few open boxes littered the floor. They were half-filled with manila folders. No doubt medical cases her mom was studying.

To someone who didn't know their past, there was no sign that there had once been a girl living here. Besides the holes in the walls that had been made by thumbtacks used to hang up the most popular boy band's poster, Georgia's memory had been completely wiped from this house.

Hannah's stomach soured, so she turned and made her way to her door. Reaching out, she turned the handle. As the door swung open, her breath caught in her throat. Nothing had changed. Everything was still in the same place. Even down to the prom dress she'd worn that night. However, it was no longer crumbled on the floor, but picked up and draped on the faded floral armchair.

Her feet made no noise as she walked across the cream-colored carpet. Itching for a shower, she grabbed her toiletries and headed to the adjoining bathroom. She flipped on the shower and steam filled the air as she undressed. Stepping into the hot water, she allowed it to roll through her hair and down her back.

Fifteen minutes later, she was clean and dry. Back in her room, she slipped into her satin pajamas and looked around. Just as she thought, her bed was still covered with all the stuffed animals she'd collected over the years. Memories of a happier time when her parents were together and her mother didn't hate her.

The urge to run away from her past filled her chest. She swallowed and turned to the window. Toward the only place she'd been able to disappear to as a child. Grinning, she unlocked the latch and slid the window open. She glanced down at the roof of the deck below her. She swung her leg over the window and slipped out.

When her feet landed on the shingles, she took a deep breath. The air had cooled. The ocean could be seen in the distance. She sat on the roof and tucked her feet underneath her. Out here, she felt free.

"Wow. It's been awhile," a deep voice said.

Her heart picked up speed as she whipped her head to the side. Logan sat, leaning against his house with a smile playing on his lips. Their decks ran parallel with each other and ever since they were kids, this was their secret hangout spot.

He leaned forward, resting his elbows on his folded knees. "I thought you might come out here."

Hannah stilled her pounding heart. "You were waiting for me?"

His face grew serious for a moment, as if there was something he wanted to say, but then he shook his head. "It's been an emotional day for you. I figured you would need to escape."

"You know me well." She shot him a smile, and his gaze softened. His familiar blue eyes stared into hers. Heat raced to her cheeks, and she cursed them. The final rays of the sun danced across his face. She hated what seeing him did to her insides.

After a few seconds, he cleared his throat. "How'd it go?"

She was thankful he decided to change the subject. "How did what go?"

"The reunion? With your mom?"

Logan was the only person who understood her relationship with her mother. He'd been there through everything. The divorce. Georgia. Everything. It felt odd and familiar to sit across from him. Part of her had longed for it. The other part feared it. Her stomach twisted. This was how her heartbreak had started—with her trusting him.

"Better than with you."

He smiled. "You mean your suitcase didn't self-combust at the hospital?" he asked.

She giggled. This was the Logan she remembered. "Nah. Apparently, fate decided to leave that tidbit for you."

"I'm lucky."

She chuckled as she studied him. What did that mean? "Yeah, it's been awhile since you've seen my underwear, huh."

Even in the encroaching darkness, she could see him blush. "They're definitely not the My Little Pony pair I flew from the flagpole at camp that summer."

Hannah laughed. She'd been so mad at him when he did that. Especially since she had been trying to impress Patrick, the cute guy that was visiting his grandmother. "Agh, you made me so mad that summer."

Logan grinned. "You were trying to impress that guy. What was his name? Paul?"

"Patrick."

Logan clapped his hands. "Patrick, that's right. Patrick the jerk. I couldn't believe he cheated on you."

"Well, cheated might be a little bit of a stretch. He only kissed me, and then I found him kissing another girl."

Logan stretched out his legs as he leaned back on his hands. "Regardless, that jerk should have known not to kiss you and then leave you like that. So not cool."

Hannah pinched her lips together as she studied Logan.

His gaze fell to her as the air grew silent. Suddenly, his

eyebrows shot up. It seemed that the memory of prom night finally caught up with him. He opened his lips as if he wanted to say something, but Hannah wasn't sure she wanted to hear it.

"It's okay. It wasn't like we were serious or anything." She needed to change the subject before tears welled up again. "So, is Tim or Bobby staying with you guys?" Logan's two younger brothers were always bothering them growing up.

"Nope. Tim's in grad school, and Bobby..." Logan's voice trailed off.

Her eyes widened. "What happened to Bobby?"

Logan cleared his throat and glanced over to the setting sun. "He died five years ago."

Her heart ached. "He did?"

Logan nodded. "Yeah. Car accident. It's been really hard on Mom and his little family."

All Hannah could do was nod as she glanced down the kitchen window where light spilled onto the ground below. That little girl from earlier must be Bobby's girl. What an awful thing to have happen to a family. She hated the silence that surrounded them so decided to change the subject. "Did you get into Notre Dame like you'd always wanted?"

His face steeled as he glanced out to the ocean. "Nah. I never left. I stayed to take care of my mom and Piper."

Her heart felt as if it would burst. What an amazing uncle he was. Taking care of his deceased brother's daughter. Just as she opened her mouth to speak, her phone rang. "Hang on," she said as she reached into her pocket, but Logan didn't seem to notice. He, too, was pulling out his phone.

LOGAN

Logan tried to focus on Jimmy's words, but his gaze kept

slipping back to Hannah. He tried to ignore the way her brow furrowed as she stared at the roof, nodding her head. He tried to ignore the way his heart pounded as he remembered the kiss they'd shared seven years ago. It was still as fresh in his mind as if it had happened yesterday.

"So, yeah, Doc says I'm gonna be out of commission up until the wedding. Something about major road rash and skin needing to heal," Jimmy said.

Logan dropped his gaze from Hannah. "Dude, why were you boarding days before your wedding?" He'd roll his eyes at his best friend's choices, but the truth was, he wasn't at all surprised.

Jimmy's raspy laugh filled the air. "You know I can't stay away—"

"Or grow up!" Sandy called out in the background.

"Sandy with you?" Logan asked.

"Yep. She still has to head out of town for the next few days. Apparently, jewelry can't wait until after our wedding—"

"Don't even start. Your boarding is what got us into this mess!" Logan could hear the bite in Sandy's voice as if she were standing right next to him.

Logan laughed. They fought like an old married couple. "What do you need, man?"

Jimmy sighed. "What I need—"

"Is to grow up!" Sandy jumped in.

There was a scraping noise followed by Jimmy's muffled voice. "Will you knock it off? How am I going to ask him with you piping up all the time behind me?"

More scraping and more muffled voices. Logan waited, allowing his gaze to fall back on Hannah who was smiling as she held the phone up to her cheek.

"Sorry. She's agreed to be quiet. There were things I

needed to get done while she was gone, but now it's against doctor's orders. Would you be willing to do them for me?"

Logan swallowed. He was never good at wedding planning stuff. When he had his shotgun wedding with Charity, she took care of all the details. "I don't know, man. I'm not that—"

"Don't worry. Sandy's asking her maid of honor to help."

Logan laughed. "I get to hang out with Patricia?" He and Jimmy used to drive her crazy as kids, getting into all of her makeup and painting faces on their baseballs.

"Nope. Patricia got shingles. Did I not tell you? Apparently, Sandy got someone else to step in."

Logan leaned back on an elbow. "Oh, really. And who's that?"

"Hannah."

His gaze whipped to her face just as her gaze did the same. Her lips mirrored his as they studied each other. Almost as if someone had said the same thing to her.

"I don't know..."

"Doctor's here. I gotta go. I'll email you the information."

"Jimmy, I—"

"Thanks! You really are an awesome best man!"

The phone fell silent. Logan pulled it from his cheek and glanced down. The picture of Piper holding up a fish greeted him. Jimmy was gone. His stomach twisted as he feared Hannah's gaze. He swallowed and looked over. Hannah's phone rested next to her, and her arms were wrapped around her raised knees.

"Sandy call you?"

She pinched her lips together and nodded. "Yep. You?"

"That was Jimmy." He slipped his phone into his pocket as silence fell around them. He wished he could read her mind. It would be nice to know what she was thinking. Then their previous conversation flooded back to him. Maybe not. He wasn't sure he wanted to learn just how much she hated him.

His phone chimed, so he pulled it back out. It was the email from Jimmy. He clicked on it and read the list. He was going to need to get the playlist to the band, grab the tuxedos, and pick up Sandy's dress. He stared at the list. Had they done nothing in preparation?

When he glanced back up to Hannah, he saw that she, too, was staring at her phone.

"Seriously? I have to pick up Sandy's dress?"

He snorted. "I'm grabbing Jimmy's tux."

Her gaze met his as she smiled. His heart skipped a beat from the way her skin crinkled around her eyes. "Did they do nothing to prepare?"

"It's Sandy and Jimmy. They've always done things by the seat of their pants."

Hannah glanced down at her phone. "Yeah, I get that. But this is just sad!" She motioned to the glowing screen.

Logan shrugged. He'd learned to accept it by now. "It'll be fun."

The look on her face told him that she doubted that.

He cleared his throat. He was desperate for her to tell him that she forgave him. "How hard can it be to spend the next day with me?"

Her lips parted as she studied him. Silence engulfed the air once more. He shot her a peace-offering smile. Why wasn't she saying anything? Had he messed things up that bad?

A small smile tugged at her lips. "I guess not *that* bad."

Relief filled his chest as he glanced down at the time. Crap. He needed to tuck Piper into bed. "Whew. You had me worried there for a moment."

She stood and brushed off the back of her pants. "Why?

We were friends once. I can't imagine why we couldn't be again."

His ears pricked at the word *friends*. She smiled and turned, slipping back into her room. He stayed until she closed her window and pulled the drapes closed.

Back in his room, he did the same. He paused as he took a deep breath. If being friends was what she needed, he'd do that. He would smile and fake that he wasn't heartbroken about what had happened between them. He'd ignore the feeling in his gut that told him he wanted so much more.

CHAPTER SEVEN

HANNAH

Hannah tried to ignore the bright red numbers that were glowing from the clock beside her. Seven in the morning, which was six Ohio time. Why couldn't she sleep?

She groaned and flipped to her side. Toward the window she'd slipped through last night. Toward Logan Blake's house. She chewed her lip as she flipped back over.

Why had she allowed herself to open up to him? Talking and laughing with him felt as natural as breathing. Why couldn't her broken heart remember how much it had hurt when he betrayed her?

Giving up on trying to sleep, Hannah flung the comforter from her body and sat up. Might as well get on with the day. She had some wedding planning to attend to. Why did Sandy think this was a good idea?

After she slipped on her Bugs Bunny slippers, she padded over to the bathroom and shut the door. Fifteen minutes later, she emerged feeling much more refreshed. Her blonde hair was pulled up into a bun, and she'd put on her standard eyeliner with mascara. Once dressed, she headed down the stairs.

In the kitchen, she pulled open the fridge. The contents were about as pretentious as her mother. Plain Greek yogurt? Egg whites? Nonfat sour cream? She pushed the contents around. Bleh. What was with her mother and fat? Perhaps that's why she was perpetually upset— she needed fat in her life.

Sighing, she shut the fridge door. There was no way she'd feel satisfied eating anything in there. Her gaze landed on her phone. She contemplated calling Bert to see if he could take her for some doughnuts. Was it too early to call for a cab?

She picked up and set down her phone about twenty times before she shook her head and turned from the counter. There was no need to bother him. He was probably sleeping. Besides, coffee would work for now.

Her mom walked in just as she was filling her mug. She was dressed in her standard blue scrubs. Hannah cleared her throat. She wasn't quite sure what to say.

"Sleep good?" her mom asked as she grabbed the coffeepot and filled up a mug.

Hannah nodded. Good, Mom was the first to break the silence. "Yeah, I guess."

Her mom replaced the pot and turned, leaning against the counter. "Well, I'm going to be pretty busy these next few days. Dr. Porter is expecting and could have the baby any minute. We're all having to pitch in to help."

Hannah held her cup. Typical. "I understand."

Her mom glanced over to her. "I'm happy you're here. I really want to work on our relationship." She gave Hannah a small smile.

Relief flitted through her stomach. If Hannah were honest with herself, that was what she wanted as well. "Me, too."

Her mom finished her coffee and then brought the mug over to the sink and rinsed it out. "Perfect. Well, I should go."

"Have a good day," Hannah called out to her mom's retreating frame. Mom raised her hand and waved, then shut the door behind her.

Hannah refilled her mug, then opened the sliding glass door and stepped out onto the deck. Three porch chairs with multicolored fabric surrounded the glass table. Pulling out a chair, she sat.

She couldn't help but smile. This was the first semi-normal conversation she'd had with her mom in a long time. For a moment, she felt hopeful. Hopeful that things could change between them. Maybe Bert was right. Christmas time was a magical time.

The sun peeked over the treetops. The air was cool and surrounded her with a salty feel. This was something she never got in Ohio. Oh, how she missed the ocean.

Leaning back, she closed her eyes.

"Excuse me," a small voice said.

Opening her eyes, she glanced up. The curly-haired girl from the Blakes' residence stared over at her. Hannah cleared her throat and sat up. "Sorry." Wait. Why was she saying sorry? This was her house. Well, her mom's house.

The little girl gave her a pointed look. "Who are you?" She took a step onto the deck. Her princess sneakers lit up in the diminishing shadows.

Hannah eyed her. "Hannah."

The little girl crossed the deck and stopped in front of a metal can. "Oh. I'm Piper." She flipped her hair over her shoulder as she pulled hard on the lid. It wouldn't budge.

"What are you doing, Piper?" Hannah couldn't help but smile. This girl reminded her of herself. Blunt and to the point. It was refreshing.

"Ms. Bell pays me to fill her birdfeeders."

Glancing around the yard, Hannah located the hanging feeders in the trees. "Oh. You can reach those?"

Piper gave her a pointed look again. "I'm seven. I'm not a baby."

Hannah gave her a serious look. "Of course, you're not. I just—"

"I know what I'm doing. I use a ladder and everything." She nodded over to the folded step stool. Then she leaned over. "And she pays me a dollar a day to do it." Her lips twitched into a smile.

"Well, that's pretty awesome," Hannah said.

Piper nodded. After a few tugs on the lid, it finally relented. She reached down and grabbed a small shovel. After the pail was full, she grabbed the stool, and headed toward the birdfeeders.

Hannah watched as she rose up onto her tippy-toes to unhook one. Then, she'd remove the top and fill it with the seeds. Half the food ended up on the ground, but she worked until they were all finished. When she climbed back onto the deck, she put everything away. Once the lid was replaced, she glanced over at Hannah.

"Why are you here?"

Hannah shifted in her seat. "Ms. Bell is my mom."

Piper narrowed her eyes. "Why haven't I ever seen you before?"

"I—um..." Hannah wasn't sure how to answer that.

Suddenly, Piper's face saddened. "I don't see my mom a lot, either. She's really busy." She dug at the wood slat with the toe of her shoe.

"Piper, I'm so sorry."

She nodded as she kept her gaze down. Hannah wished

there was something she could say that would help her feel better. "Is your mom gone a lot?"

Piper nodded.

Hannah leaned in. "Mine too."

Piper's bright blue eyes rose to meet hers. "Wanna know a secret?"

Hannah gave her a small smile and nodded. "Of course."

"I'm saving my money for when my mom comes to visit. She promised to take me to the American Girl Doll store once she's saved up some money." Piper giggled. "I'm going to surprise her with what I earn here and at my grandma's. I just hope it will be enough to get her to come."

"That's so sweet. Your mom's a lucky lady to have you as a daughter." Inside, her heart broke. What kind of mom abandoned her daughter like that? Especially after losing her spouse. Hannah gave Piper a wide smile. "You know, I loved the American Girl dolls growing up. In fact, I have some of the original dolls upstairs in my room."

Piper's eyes widened as she glanced toward the house. "Really?"

"Yeah. Maybe, sometime, I can show them to you."

Piper nodded her head. "Yes! I can bring my dolls and we can play together."

"Sounds like a date."

"Piper?"

Hannah's heart sped at the sound of Logan's voice.

"Piper? Where are you?"

"Talking to Miss Hannah," Piper called out as she twirled around on the deck.

"Oh..." Logan's voice grew louder as he neared. His blue eyes met Hannah's, and her resolve to forget her past feelings for him dissolved. "Why are you bugging Miss Hannah?"

"Actually, I was bugging her. She was over here doing her job." Hannah raised her eyebrow at Logan.

He nodded. "Well, Grandma Blake is waiting with a full dishwasher. Said she'll pay fifty cents to anyone willing to unload it. I figured I'd give you first dibs."

Piper sprinted down the steps. "I've got it!" she called. Her voice grew faint the farther she got.

Hannah smiled as she watched her disappear. "She's a sweet girl."

Logan nodded. "Yeah. We're lucky to have her around. My mom loves it." His voice had softened so Hannah peeked over to him. There was something there. A sadness in his stance that made her wonder what had happened.

"It must be good for her. You know, helps with the loss."

Logan's gaze met hers and a funny look passed over his face. "Yeah. She took it the hardest when Bobby passed."

Hannah gave him a small smile. What an awful thing for a little girl to go through. "Well, it's good that you all banded together."

Logan shoved his hands into the front pockets of his jeans. "Hannah, I'm not sure—"

"What's the plan for today?" Hannah interrupted. The tone of his voice and the longing in his gaze made her stomach flip. The less they talked about their feelings the better. They had a strictly best-man-and-maid-of-honor relationship. She needed to keep that in mind.

Logan pulled out his phone from his back pocket. After a few seconds, he spoke. "We have to finalize the songs with the band and pick up the dress and tuxedos."

"I still can't believe we are doing this for them."

Logan returned his phone to his pocket and nodded. "I've gotten used to it. Last year, while they were on a cruise, they had me give their dog a bath for a dog show they'd entered it into, but forgot about when they booked their tickets."

"Oh, really?"

Logan nodded. "Yeah. Worst part? I was the guy who had to show the dog."

Hannah burst out laughing. The image of Logan running sprints across a dog obstacle course was too much.

Logan smiled. "Hey, now. We won."

Hannah's sides hurt. "You're a jack of all trades. So talented."

His cheeks reddened as his gaze swept over her. For a moment, there was happiness that surrounded them. This was so familiar. And Hannah's heart ached for the familiarity.

Logan's face stilled. "We should probably get going."

Hannah nodded as she stood. "Let me grab my shoes, and I'll be right back." She grabbed her mug and headed into the house. As she rinsed her cup out at the sink, her thoughts turned to Logan. How was she going to survive the day with him when the butterflies swarming in her stomach wouldn't go away?

LOGAN

Logan settled down on the deck chair that Hannah had just vacated. His thoughts flew around in his mind. She'd met Piper. They'd talked. He wasn't sure how he felt about it. For a moment, it seemed as if he was going to be able to confess to Hannah just what had happened on prom night. But she always changed the subject.

He scrubbed the stubble on his chin with his hand. Once the story was finally out in the open, he'd feel better. But he wasn't going to push her. They'd get there in time.

His phone chimed. Glancing down, he scrolled through his messages.

Sandy says the dress shop opens at eight-thirty. But the tuxedos won't be ready until ten. Think you can make that?

Logan inwardly groaned, but answered, *Will do.*

His heart pounded harder at the thought of spending the day with Hannah. Their conversation last night left him wanting more. More memories relived, more laughs, more... kisses. He still remembered the feeling of her lips on his.

"I'm ready," her soft voice said from behind him.

He jumped and turned. His heart sped from the way the sun lit up behind her. Afraid that his voice would betray him, he just nodded.

They walked to his car in silence. She shot quizzical glances his way. When their gaze met, he smiled.

"I got a text from Jimmy," he said as he pulled the door open for her.

She nodded as she climbed in. "What did he say?"

Logan shut the door and jogged around to the driver's side. "We need to grab the dress at eight thirty and then the tux at ten." He started up the car and *Jingle Bells* blared through his speaker. Piper had insisted on Christmas music on the way home from Girl Scouts last night. He peeked sheepishly over at Hannah as he reached over and turned it down. "Sorry."

She smiled. "I love this song. You can leave it."

The music filled the cab as Logan drove down the street. From the corner of his eye, he saw Hannah's shoulders relax.

"It's romantic," she said, her voice almost a whisper.

"What is?"

"Getting married at Christmastime." She wrapped her arms around her chest as she stared out the window. He knew that stance. She was attempting to protect herself. How could he show her that she could trust him?

Hannah shifted and pressed her hand against her stomach. "Do you think it might be possible to stop by Little Mama's bakery?"

Logan glanced over at her. "You're hungry? Did you not get breakfast?"

She shook her head. "Nope. My mom seems to have gotten rid of every fatty food there is. I'm starving."

"You've got it." He flipped on his blinker and merged into the left lane. Three minutes later, he pulled into the parking lot. He opened the door and the smell of fried food wafted around him. His stomach grumbled in response.

He waited for her to round the hood of the truck and then he fell into step with her on the way to the bakery's door. As he reached out to grab the handle, Hannah did the same. His fingers brushed hers and tingles erupted from the touch. He swallowed and glanced down at her.

"I'm... sorry," she whispered, her gaze meeting his.

She was close. So close. If he wanted to, he could reach out and embrace her. And for a moment, the look in her eye told him that's what she wanted as well.

But just as quickly as the moment had happened, it disappeared. Hannah cleared her throat and stepped back. "You first," she said as she pulled her purse strap higher up on her shoulder.

Logan pulled the door open. "After you."

She hesitated, then walked into the bakery. Logan paused as he glanced down the road, hoping to gather his emotions. Feeling like an idiot, he rolled his shoulders and followed after Hannah. He needed to get a grip, and now.

CHAPTER EIGHT

LOGAN

After Hannah paid, Logan placed his order for a cream-filled long john. The peppy girl behind the counter smiled widely at him as she placed the doughnut down. He wasn't in the mood to flirt, so he nodded and grabbed it. The wrapper crinkled under his fingertips.

When he turned, he zoned in on Hannah who'd sat down at the table situated against the window. The sun burst through the glass and surrounded her. His heart sped up as he approached. From the way emotions raced through his body, Logan knew he was in trouble.

The legs of the chair made a scraping noise as he pulled it out and sat down. Hannah's raspberry-filled doughnut was half gone.

Her eyes danced with the smile she was hiding behind her hand. "Sorry," she said as she grabbed a nearby napkin and wiped her mouth. "I couldn't wait."

SECOND CHANCE WITH THE BILLIONAIRE   59

Logan shrugged. "Nope, I get it." He took a huge bite of his doughnut.

They sat in silence until they were finished. Logan wiped his fingers and lips.

Hannah glanced around. "I'm going to go to the bathroom, and then we can head out."

He nodded. "Sounds good."

"Watch my stuff?" she asked as she motioned to her wallet and phone.

"Sure." He pulled it close to him.

Hannah pushed her chair back and headed to the bathroom.

Logan leaned back and folded his arms. As much as he wanted to tell himself that his stomach was in knots from the sugar in the pastry, he knew that wasn't the case. He leaned his elbows on the tabletop and bowed his head. He needed to get a grip.

The table began to vibrate. Then a blaring song sounded as Hannah's phone lit up. Logan grabbed it. Half the occupants milling around the shop stopped to stare at him. His face heated as he gave them a sheepish grin. Why was her phone so loud?

He swiped the screen, desperate to get the loud, twangy country song to quit. The image of a guy in a suit greeted him. Logan stared at it. Next to his image was a text. As much as he tried not to read it, he couldn't help himself.

Just wondering where you are and if you've thought about my proposal. I love you and can't wait until you're Mrs. Samson Price. Call me when you get this.

Logan swallowed as he located the volume button on the side of the phone and turned the ringer to vibrate. He hit the power button and the image of Samson and his declaration of love faded into darkness.

Hannah had a boyfriend? Why hadn't she told him? From the looks of that text, they were pretty serious. Proposal? He set the phone down on her wallet and turned his gaze outside. He was such a fool. Of course, Hannah would move on. It wasn't like he hadn't. He had married and divorced.

"Ready?" Hannah's sweet voice asked from behind him.

He nodded and stood. "Yeah. They're opening in a few minutes."

She grabbed her wallet and phone. "Let's get going then."

He tried not to stare at her as she lifted her phone and swiped it on. Her forehead crinkled as she paused. He knew she was reading the text. Why wasn't she saying anything?

"Important?" He pushed the door open and nodded to her phone.

Hannah pressed the button and dropped it into her purse. Her cheeks were flushed as she walked through the door. "Nope. Nothing important."

Logan studied her. Why was she acting so weird? What was the story between her and Samson? Did she not want to marry him? Did he dare hope?

They climbed into his truck, and he started it up. The drive to the bridal shop was silent. Logan wanted to ask her about Samson, but he didn't want to reveal that he'd read the text. Why couldn't he just ask her? They'd been friends once. He could ask her as a friend. Right?

He finally got the nerve to open his lips as he parked his truck, but Hannah didn't wait. She opened her door and jumped out. She was agitated. Did she suspect that he'd seen?

She disappeared into the bridal shop as Logan climbed down. The only thing he knew right now was—he couldn't move forward until he knew.

HANNAH

A woman in a black suit stood behind the counter at the bridal shop. She was busy tapping on a keyboard in front an aged monitor. Her hair was pulled back into a tight bun and a pair of reading glasses hung around her neck. Hannah approached and waited. Cutout snowflakes hung from the ceiling and spun in the cool air that burst from the vent.

After a few minutes, Hannah cleared her throat. "Excuse me?"

The woman lifted her finger, but didn't break her concentration. Hannah pinched her lips shut. What was she supposed to do now?

Finally, the clicking stopped, and she turned. "Sorry, sweetie. If I get interrupted, I forget, and I needed to get that order in." She smiled. "When's the big day?"

The clanging of the bells hanging from the door drew her attention away from Hannah. They both turned to see Logan slip into the shop.

"Is that the lucky fellow?" The shop lady gave Hannah an approving look.

"Um, no. We're not getting married." Her stomach flitted at the thought of her marrying Logan Blake.

The woman smiled. "I'm sorry. But I must say, you would make an adorable couple."

This conversation needed to change. "Okay. I'm actually here to pick up a dress for my friend, Sandy Young?"

The woman turned back to the computer and started typing again. Thankfully, it only lasted about a minute.

"Yes, I see that. We have the dress in the back."

Hannah nodded. "Great."

The woman disappeared through the door behind her. Hannah turned and leaned against the counter. Logan was wandering around, staring at the different dresses that hung on racks next to the dressing rooms.

She chewed her lip as she watched him. Had he seen Samson's text? Ugh, why hadn't she just brought her phone with her? She didn't think Samson would try to contact her right now. Not after she'd told him she needed some time. She pulled out her phone and turned it on.

Mrs. Samson Price stared back at her.

She didn't know what she wanted.

"Here it is, dear," the woman said as she walked through the back door. When she went to lift it over the counter for Hannah, she paused. "Wait a minute." Taking the dress back, she stared at it. "Oh, no."

Hannah shut off her phone and shoved it into her back pocket. "What's wrong?"

The woman glanced at her from over the dress. "I'm so sorry, but apparently, the work order got damaged and the measurements for height got removed. This dress is not hemmed."

Hannah stared at her. "What?"

"Is there anyway the bride could come in for a fitting? We can get it to her for the wedding."

"Um..."

"What's the problem?" Logan asked as he approached.

"Apparently, this dress is not hemmed. They need Sandy to come in."

Logan glanced at her, then back to the woman behind the counter. "She's out of town until the wedding day."

The woman's lips fluttered like a fish out of water. "Um... well..."

Hannah pulled out her phone and hit Sandy's picture.

Dress is not hemmed. They lost your measurements. What do you want me to do?

She hit send and waited. Both Logan and the shop worker stared at her. Finally, after what felt like an eternity, her phone vibrated. Huh, she could have sworn she had the ringer turned up.

WHAT!!! Are you serious?

Hannah nodded at her phone, even though Sandy couldn't see her. *Yep.*

Ahh! That's so frustrating. You're going to have to try it on for me.

Hannah's cheeks heated. That was the last thing she wanted to do. Trying on a wedding dress went against her resolve to forget about weddings—to forget about Samson's proposal.

Um... Do you think that will be okay?

Her phone vibrated much quicker this time.

It'll be fine. Thanks for being such an awesome friend!

Hannah sighed and clicked her phone off.

"Get me a dressing room," she said to the woman behind the counter.

In under two minutes, Hannah found herself standing in a bright white dressing room, staring at Sandy's wedding dress. It was covered completely in lace. The neckline curved down, and it had capped sleeves. If she were honest with herself, this would be the dress she would have picked. Crap.

"Do you need some help?" the woman behind the counter asked.

Hannah eyed the pearl buttons down the back. "Yeah."

She nodded and shut the door, but not before Hannah caught a glimpse of Logan as he sat down on the plush pink couch next to the three full-length mirrors.

"My name's Thelma," she said as she pulled the dress off the hook.

"Hannah," she said as she slipped off her shirt. Might as well get to know Thelma, especially since she'd be seeing Hannah in her underwear in a matter of seconds. But apparently, that was Hannah's new thing. People seeing her undergarments.

Once the dress was on, Hannah knew right away this was a mistake. It hugged her in all the right places. The bodice was fitted all the way past her hips. Then it flared out at the bottom. She reached up and released her curls from her bun. They cascaded down her back.

"It looks like this dress was made for you," Thelma said with her eyes wide.

Hannah pinched her lips and nodded. Thelma was right. Too bad it was Sandy's.

"Yeah," Hannah whispered. Then she straightened. Best to get it off before she became too attached. "Let's hem this dress and get it over with."

Thelma nodded and opened the door.

Butterflies erupted in Hannah's stomach. The look on Logan's face made her heart pound so hard, she could hear it in her ears. His eyes were wide as his gaze swept over her.

She grabbed the bottom of the dress and walked from the dressing room. As if from instinct, Logan stood.

"Hannah, you look..." His voice was low.

She cursed her heated cheeks and kept her gaze on the ground as she walked past him. Thelma waved her over to the pedestal in the center of the room. Hannah grabbed the skirt with her hand and swung her foot up onto the pedestal. While the dress was beautiful, they really didn't design it for a woman to move in. She teetered as she tried to straighten.

Suddenly, a warm hand grabbed hers and another hand slid around her waist.

"Whoa," Logan's deep voice whispered into her ear. "I've got you." He held onto her until she was stabilized on the stand. His hands remained for a second longer than needed.

"I'm okay. Thanks," she said, cursing her emotion-filled

voice that exposed her.

When she turned away from him, she caught Thelma's gaze and Thelma smiled.

"What?" Hannah asked.

Thelma knelt down in front of her. "You sure you aren't a couple?"

Hannah laughed, which came out more like a wheeze. "Me and Logan? Of course not. We're friends."

Thelma shoved some pins in her mouth and then began tucking the dress up. "Honey, I've seen lots of couples come in and out of this place." She moved the pins to the side of her lips as she spoke. "You have some of the strongest chemistry I've ever seen."

Hannah's gaze whipped to Logan who'd gone back to the couch. His elbows were on his knees and a bridal magazine was spread open in front of him. It seemed as if he were trying a bit too hard to read the pages.

Could he hear Thelma? What was she supposed to say to that?

"It's over. It's in the past. We've both moved on," Hannah said. Logan's shoulders stiffened, and she dropped her gaze. The words didn't taste good on her tongue. But what else was she supposed to say?

Thelma smiled. "Okay, sweetie. If you say so."

The Christmas ballad that played over the speakers filled the silent air. Thelma's words rolled around in Hannah's mind. Why didn't Thelma believe her? Hannah was over Logan. In fact, she had a proposal waiting for her in Ohio. She wanted to tell that to Thelma. Prove to her that she really was over Logan.

But she doubted that Thelma would listen. And in the end, maybe Thelma was right. There was chemistry there, and it scared and excited her at the same time.

CHAPTER NINE

LOGAN

Logan stared at a picture of different-colored stiletto shoes, trying to ignore the conversation that was taking place between the shop woman and Hannah. He was also trying to ignore the pain in his gut from Hannah's words. *It's over. It's in the past.*

Ouch.

Maybe she really was getting married to this Samson guy. Maybe things really were over. As much as he wanted to say that he had no feelings for her whatsoever, he knew that wasn't true. They had a history. But maybe that was all. A past. That was all they shared. He needed to get over whatever he was feeling and soon.

Flipping the magazine closed, he placed it next to him and sat up, leaning back on the couch. The shop owner had stood and was circling Hannah, who had her arms folded. Her gaze followed the woman.

"I think that will do," she said, nodding in Hannah's direction.

A look of relief flashed over Hannah's face. "Great. Now, can I get out of this?"

The woman nodded, and Hannah reached out her hand, and she was helped down.

"Great. I can't wait to get this dress off."

Ten minutes later, Hannah emerged from the dressing room in her sweatshirt and jeans. Her hair was back up in a bun, and she looked comfortable.

They nodded to the woman who had taken up residence at the counter again.

"It was very nice to meet you two," she called after them. "Come back once you make it official!" They closed the door on her words.

Logan's face heated as he glanced over to Hannah. She looked about as uncomfortable as he felt. They climbed into his truck. The silence around them was about as palpable as the air before a summer storm.

He started up the truck and backed out of the parking lot.

"That was awkward." Hannah's voice broke through the music that carried from his speakers.

He let out the breath he was holding. Thank goodness she'd spoken first. "Right?"

Hannah giggled, and the tension dissipated. "Why would she ever think we could be a couple? I've moved on. You've moved on. It's been seven years. There's nothing there anymore. We're just old friends. Siblings, even."

Logan gripped the steering wheel. Well, that's not what he would classify them as. Really? Her brother? He flipped on his blinker and merged into another lane. "Most older women love to play matchmaker."

Hannah snorted. "Yeah, well, she should probably keep her focus more on not losing measurements then predicting people's love life."

Ooh, knife to the gut. Was hearing about a relationship with him really that bad? There was a bite to Hannah's tone that caused him to shift in his seat.

When Hannah didn't say anything more, he glanced over to her. Her gaze met his, and her expression softened. "I'm sorry. I didn't mean for that to come out that way. It's just... all this wedding stuff makes me uncomfortable. It's bringing out a side of me that's ugly. It's not your fault, and it's not Thelma's fault, either."

Logan nodded. Well, at least she felt bad about insulting him. That did help.

He pulled up in front of the tuxedo rental store and turned. "I'll be just a minute. Hopefully, they didn't lose any measurements as well." Hannah nodded as he jumped from the cab.

In under five minutes, he finished with the man at the register and returned with a handful of tuxedos.

Hannah raised her eyebrows. "That was fast."

Logan nodded as he buckled. "Women always take longer. Didn't you know that?"

She giggled as he pulled from the parking spot. "Yeah, you're right."

He was enjoying the sound of her laugh. He wanted to make her happy. "This one time, Charity took so long to get ready that I actually fell asleep on the couch. Like, mouth open kind of sleep. When she woke me up, I had to change because I had a drool spot on my shirt."

Hannah laughed again. "I can imagine that." Then she grew quiet. "Who's Charity?"

"My ex," Logan said, then pinched his lips. It was an instinct. He glanced over to Hannah, who had her eyes wide.

"Ex? Girlfriend?"

Logan focused on the road. "Wife."

"Wow. When did you get married?" She paused. "And divorced?"

Well, might as well tell her. "Right out of high school. Remember Charity Monson?"

"The cheerleading captain? You married her?"

Logan fiddled with the radio settings. "Yep."

Hannah grew quiet again, so Logan peeked over to her. She had a look that he couldn't quite read.

"It didn't last long. After a few years, we discovered we weren't compatible together." He never liked it when his friends bad-mouthed their exes, and vowed to never do that to Charity. Saying they split because they weren't working out wasn't a lie. It just wasn't the whole truth.

"Well, you were young." She paused. "Charity Monson? Huh. Never would have put you two together." She picked a piece of thread off her pants.

"What about you? Any ex-husbands lurking in your past?" He eyed her, hoping she'd give him a clue about Samson. How serious were they?

Hannah laughed. "No. No, ex-husbands for me. Just ex-boyfriends."

Political answer. "What about almost ex-husbands? Any of those?" This was her moment. He was handing her the opportunity to tell him about Samson.

Silence. The light in front of him turned red so he stopped, then took this moment to turn and look at her.

"No almost proposals?" Logan asked

Ouch. She didn't trust him enough to tell him about Samson. He sighed. Maybe he deserved it. He did run out on her on prom night. But how could he go back onto the dance floor after they'd kissed and tell Hannah that he'd gotten Charity pregnant? Especially when he knew the right thing to do was to marry Charity. Would Hannah have understood?

He gripped the steering wheel tighter. Perhaps. But he was just a kid, and he acted on instinct. He had no idea that she'd pack up and leave the next day, never to see him again. If he could go back in time, he would have handled things differently. He would have been honest. But now, the result of his deception was more deception.

Their relationship status was his fault. He squared his shoulders as he pulled into the parking lot of the local recording studio. If there was one thing he was going to do this Christmas, it was mending their relationship. He'd earn her trust back one way or another.

HANNAH

Logan put the car into park and smiled over at Hannah. She returned even though her stomach was in knots. Why didn't she just confess about Samson?

"Jimmy sent me the playlist. All we have to do is go in and give the list to the band. Then our job as runaround slaves is finished." He grabbed the door handle and pulled it open.

"Sounds good." Although being done meant heading back home. Which also meant sitting alone in her mom's house with nonfat ice cream. With the way she was feeling, she needed the full-fat stuff.

"All righty. Let's do this," he said as he jumped from the cab and slammed the door.

Hannah did the same. As they walked to the entrance of the studio, she took a deep breath. Ever since she had Sandy's wedding dress on, her emotions were frazzled. She needed to get a grip. Rolling her shoulders back, she smiled. She decided to push the thoughts and decisions about Samson to the back of her mind and deal with them later.

Logan held the door and waved her in. A girl with tattoos

SECOND CHANCE WITH THE BILLIONAIRE   71

on her arms was sitting at a desk on the far side of the room. She was bobbing her head to some rock music that blared from the speakers next to the monitor. She turned when they approached.

"Logan! How's it going?" she asked as she stood and pulled him into a hug.

Hannah studied them. Who was this woman?

When they pulled apart, the girl glanced over to her. "Who's this?"

Logan stepped back. "Sorry. Audrey, this is Hannah. Hannah, Audrey."

"Hi," Hannah said.

"Hannah, nice to meet you." She stuck out her hand.

"So, how do you know each other? I know it's not through music. Logan can't carry a tune to save his life," Hannah said as she shook Audrey's hand.

Audrey let out a deep laugh. "That's for sure."

Logan play-punched her shoulder. "Hey, now. I'm not that bad."

Audrey snorted. "When he sings, dogs whimper," she said, leaning toward Hannah.

Logan glanced over at her with a sheepish look on his face. "We're on the PTA together."

Hannah raised her eyebrows. That was not what she was expecting to hear him say. "At Piper's school?" Hannah asked. Logan was such a good uncle.

They both nodded.

"My son, Racer, is in the same class as Piper."

"Audrey's the PTA president."

Hannah nodded.

"Hey, that reminds me. I didn't see your name on the sign-up sheet for the school's Christmas party." Audrey narrowed her eyes. "You aren't bailing on me, are you, Blake?"

Logan glanced over at Hannah, then back to Audrey. "I wasn't sure how things were going to play out this Christmas."

Audrey held up her hands. "That's not an excuse. You're coming and manning the Coal Toss booth." Then her gaze landed on Hannah. "You know, it's a two-person job. One to keep the hopped-up-on-sugar kids calm and the other to collect the coal."

Hannah pointed to her chest. "Me? You want me to help?"

Audrey nodded. "Great! I'll put you both down."

Logan leaned over. "No use in arguing. Audrey always wins. That's why she's been the undefeated PTA president for five years."

"But isn't Racer only seven? She was PTA president before he was even in school?"

Logan nodded. "Exactly."

So there really was no way of getting out of this. Hannah turned and smiled. "I'll be there."

"Great!" She leaned against the desk. "So what can I help you guys with?"

Logan pulled out his phone. "Jimmy needed me to give you his song list."

Audrey nodded. "Great." She took his phone, set it on the desk, and started writing.

Hannah wandered over to the glass window that separated them from the band on the other side. The singer was holding the microphone and his eyes were closed as he wailed into it. The music was muffled as it rattled the walls.

"You like rock?" Audrey appeared next to her.

Hannah jumped. "I—um, sure."

Audrey eyed her. "Come on," she said as she opened the door, causing the music to carry out into the foyer.

"I—well—"

"Come on." Audrey waved toward the other room.

Not wanting to argue, Hannah nodded and followed her gesture.

"You, too, Blake!" Audrey yelled as they entered to other room.

Logan appeared in the doorway. "What are you guys doing?"

Audrey walked over to another door and pulled it open. The music petered off as the members took note of Audrey's presence.

"Guys, this is Jimmy's best man, Logan. And his girl-friend..." She drew out each syllable as if she were waiting for someone to correct her.

Hannah moved to correct her, but Logan interjected first. "Old friend."

"Old friend, Hannah," Audrey repeated.

The band members all nodded and said hi.

Audrey turned back to Logan and Hannah. She reached out and motioned between herself and the band. "We were having an argument earlier about a particular song. They don't think it's a fit for the wedding, but I do. When it comes to these guys, they always overrule me." She leaned over. "There's three of them and one of me. But I get two votes 'cause I run this joint."

"What do you need, Audrey?" Logan asked, eyeing her.

"I want them to play the song for you two, and you can tell me if you think that Jimmy and Sandy would like it at their wedding."

Logan studied her. "But I gave you the list."

Audrey shrugged. "Lists are more like guidelines." A triumphant smile spread across her lips as she raised her arm. "Play it." Then she wandered over to the far chair and sat down. Hannah folded her arms as she studied the band. If she were honest with herself, she was intrigued with what song had them arguing.

The drummer raised his sticks and tapped the count. The guitarist began to strum as the bass guitar joined in. Soon, the room was filled with a slow ballad.

The singer from earlier stepped up and began to sing. It was a low, soulful song.

"This a good one," Logan said as he stepped up next to her.

"I recognize it." Hannah stilled as she listened to the words.

"It's a rendition of *Perfect*, by Ed Sheeran."

"Oh." She wrapped her arms around her chest, trying to still her pounding heart. She could feel Logan's presence as he stood next to her. The memory of him wrapping his arms around her as he led her around the dance floor filled her every sense.

"Ask her to dance," Audrey called out.

Hannah whipped around to shoot her an angry look. Audrey met it with an unapologetic stare as she nodded toward the two of them.

Turning back around, her heart sank and soared at the same time. Logan's hand was extended, and he had an inviting look.

"Seems like a waste of a good song." His smiled, and melted the icy wall she was attempting to put up between them.

"I...um..." Her gaze fell behind him, toward the bright red exit sign. Perhaps she could make it there if she ran. Before she could steel her nerves enough to dash to the door, Logan's hand engulfed hers as he pulled her close.

"Logan..." she whispered as she allowed him to wrap his arm around her waist.

"It's just a dance," he said with his voice cloaked with emotion.

"I—" But all the words she could think of disappeared. He cradled her hand in his and stepped forward. Out of instinct, Hannah stepped back and within seconds, they were dancing around the recording studio.

Everything she had been holding onto faded into the song. Her body relaxed, and her soul soaked in the comfort that being in his arms gave her. This was familiar. This was safe. Her heart screamed that this was where she belonged. But her head was sending out warning signals.

"Hannah..." he whispered.

She dared exposure and glanced up. The memory of standing on the dance floor, glancing up at him as he leaned down to kiss her, flashed into her mind.

Suddenly, she didn't want to dance. Dropping his hand and stepping back, she glanced over to the exit sign. "I'm sorry," she whispered as she dropped her gaze and headed straight toward the door. Straight toward freedom.

CHAPTER TEN

LOGAN

The air felt cool in the absence of Hannah's presence. Logan watched her retreating frame. He fought every urge to run after her. From the look on her face, he knew the best thing to do right now was to give her some space. He'd do that for her.

"What was that about?" Audrey asked as she stepped up next to him.

"We have a past," Logan said.

"I'd say."

"It was my fault. I hurt her a long time ago." He shoved his hands into his front pockets. "I'm trying to get her to trust me again."

Audrey glanced over to him. "Was she the one that got away?"

He nodded. "Something like that."

She smiled. "Don't give up. If it's meant to be, it'll happen."

Logan followed after her as she left the recording studio. "But what if she's sitting on a proposal?"

Audrey narrowed her eyes. "You mean, she's been proposed to, but she hasn't answered?"

Logan nodded.

"Eh"—Audrey shrugged—"I wouldn't worry too much about it. If she hasn't said yes, she probably won't."

Logan fiddled with his phone as he thought about what she said. There was probably truth to her words. He just wished he had as much confidence as she did.

"You're a great guy, Logan. You'll do the right thing."

"Yeah." He turned his gaze toward the ground.

"Speaking of you being a great guy..." Audrey's voice drifted off.

He turned to look at her. "What?" There was a look in her eye that made him uncomfortable.

"My mom is Josie. Josie Pinkles."

Logan shrugged. "I don't know who that is."

Audrey traced her finger across a manila envelope on the desk. "She recently pitched the idea of the Kitty Cuddle to you."

The image of a woman with white hair and bright eyes entered his mind. "Oh, that's right." Then his stomach sank. Did Audrey know about his dad's money?

"Don't be mad, but she told me that you were interested in making some investments."

Logan tried to relax his face so his frustration wouldn't show through. "I'm not really sure what I'm going to do right now." How much did his mom tell Josie? Did Audrey know the dollar amount he was worth?

Audrey studied him, then nodded. "Well, I'm looking at expanding the studio to attract more bands. I'm looking for some investors. Here's my business plan and current stats." She lifted the envelope up and held it out. "Just look it over."

The earnest glint in her eyes made it impossible for Logan to say no. He nodded as he took it from her. "I'll look at it."

Audrey's face relaxed. "Great!" Then she glanced down at the playlist she'd written earlier. "I'll get this to the band."

Logan nodded. "Sounds good. I'll let Jimmy know you have it." He turned and headed toward the front door. Hopefully, he'd given Hannah enough time to cool off. He wasn't sure what he was going to say to her, but he couldn't leave her fuming outside. That wouldn't do anything for his current resolve to earn her trust.

HANNAH

Hannah stood outside the studio, pacing back and forth. Her stomach was in knots. On the one hand, she was completely embarrassed that she lost her crap inside. On the other hand, her feelings for Logan were starting to resurface. Both of those added up to an emotionally crazed Hannah.

She grabbed her phone and pushed the button with Bert's name on it.

"You've got Bert," his rough voice said after three rings.

"Bert, it's Hannah. Could you come pick me up?"

"Sure, where are you?"

"The recording studio on Fifth and Main."

He fell silent for a moment. "Yep, that should be fine. I'll be there in three minutes."

Hannah's shoulder's relaxed. "Perfect."

She threw the phone back into her purse. She peered around the building, grateful that Logan had decided to give her some space. Thankfully, he remembered she needed time to cool down. There had been plenty of times as kids she'd go running to her house upset with something he'd done. It wouldn't take her long to forgive him, but she did need that break.

Sighing, she leaned against the wall of the building. What a mess her life had become. Samson. Logan. Her mom. She was struggling to mend relationships. Heck, she was struggling to maintain relationships.

It was growing more apparent that running away wasn't the way to solve anything. She'd spent seven years apart from her mom. And that did nothing. She was still at the same place she'd been at when she left. Their relationship hadn't changed.

As much as she struggled to connect with her mom, one thing was certain, she missed her. It was hard to watch all her roommates and friends get married with their moms right alongside them. Giggling over wedding details and picking out dresses. Would she ever have that? Could her mom ever forgive her?

She tilted her face toward the sky and let the early afternoon sunlight shine on her skin. It warmed her skin. Maybe it was time she started telling the truth. Time to start fixing the things that she'd broken in her life. She wasn't a victim. She controlled her destiny.

"Hannah?" Logan's voice carried from around the building.

It started now. "I'm over here." She made her way to the front.

He rounded the corner. He raised his eyebrows as if he weren't sure what she was going to do. "You okay?"

She pinched her lips together and nodded. "Yeah." She relaxed her face, hoping to portray how she felt. "I'm really sorry for running out on you like that."

He studied her. "It's okay. You don't need to apologize. I shouldn't have asked you to dance." His voice grew softer. "We do have a history."

Her cheeks heated at the mention of their past. Squaring her shoulders, she gave him a smile. "But that's just it. It's history. We're both adults. We should be able to move forward." She reached out her hand. "To a fresh start—as friends."

He eyed her hand. "Hannah, I don't think you understand what happ—"

"I'm engaged," she blurted out.

His gaze met hers. "What?"

She fiddled with her purse strap. "I'm sorry I didn't say that earlier. It's really recent, and I've been trying to process it all." She took a deep breath. "But I'm engaged."

Logan took a step back. "To whom?"

"His name is Samson. I met him during a weekend getaway to New York. His family owns a bunch of high-rise apartments there. He moved to Ohio for some business ventures and to live closer to me."

Logan remained quiet as he watched her. Then he turned his gaze toward the ground. "I'm happy for you. Although, I'm not quite sure why you lied to me." His pain-filled gaze met hers. "We used to be so close. I just wish we could go back to that."

Clutching her strap, Hannah nodded. Truth was, she wished that as well. All she wanted to do was rewind the clock and start over. She'd make the right choices this time. "I know. I do, too. But we can't. The past can't be changed. All we can do is learn from it and move on. And I'm moving on."

He shoved his hands into his front pockets. "Does he treat you well?"

"Yeah." In all reality, their relationship was perfect. They never argued or disagreed. Most evenings they would spend time in her living room with Samson on his phone negotiating deals while she was buried in the newest case file. "He's a good guy."

Logan reached out, his fingertips inches from her arm. Her heart raced as she studied his hand. She wanted and feared his touch. A few seconds ticked by, but they felt like an eternity. Suddenly, his hand engulfed her arm. She glanced up at him and the look in his eyes took her breath away.

"I'm happy for you." His Adam's apple rose and fell. "It's all I've ever wanted for you."

"I know." She held his gaze. She wanted him to know that they were okay. Even if they missed out on being a couple, they could still be friends. She wasn't going to run again. "You were always my best friend. We will always have those memories."

They stood in silence with Logan's hand still wrapped around her arm. The breeze shook the trees, and Hannah watched as the sun danced across his face. The salty ocean air surrounded them. She took a deep breath, pushing down all the frustration she'd felt for so long.

A car's honk pulled them from the trance they were in. Hannah jumped and glanced behind Logan. Bert had pulled up in front of the building and was waving at her.

"That's my cab," she said, nodding toward Bert.

Logan's eyes narrowed as he glanced behind him. "Cab—I can take you home, Hannah."

She shook her head. "No, that's okay. I don't want to inconvenience you."

"Inconv—Hannah, it's okay." He reached out to touch her arm.

Like two magnetic sides that weren't meant to go together, Hannah pulled back. "Logan, listen, I'm engaged. Things have changed. We will always have our memories, but that's all. We need to move forward."

Logan flexed his hand and dropped it. "So moving forward means giving up on our friendship?"

Hannah shook her head. "Not giving up. Just changing it. Adapting."

He pushed his hand through his hair and nodded. "Got it."

"Logan"—she stepped toward him—"I think it's the best for both of us. Moving on is what's best."

He held up his hands. "I understand." Then he waved toward Bert. "He's waiting."

Hannah chewed her lip. Obviously, something she'd said bothered him. Why was he acting this way? He had to know that she cared about him. Right?

Bert honked again. She glanced over as he rolled the window down. "Coming, girlie? I've got other places to be."

"Hang on." She turned to Logan. "Are we okay?"

"Yep," Logan said, avoiding her gaze.

She hesitated, then turned. "I'll see you at the wedding."

"See you." He'd shoved his hands back into his front pockets and stared out into the brush.

Hannah hated leaving him like this. He was upset about something. But she wasn't sure what. They'd talked about personal stuff. That had to appease him.

She pulled open the car door and slipped onto the seat. When she shut her door, Bert drove away.

"Who was that?" he asked from the front seat.

Hannah steeled her nerves and glanced back at Logan. He was watching the cab pull away. There was a pained expression on his face. She'd hurt him, but she didn't know how.

"That was Logan."

"Logan? Is he the long-lost love?"

Hannah's cheeks heated. "He was the past love."

Bert nodded. "I've still got it," he mumbled to himself as he flipped on his blinker and merged onto the freeway. "You guys seemed to be having a moment."

Hannah let out a breath as she watched the trees whip past her. "Yeah. I was saying things that needed to be said."

Bert nodded again. "All good. How'd he take it?"

Logan's pained gaze entered Hannah's mind. "I'm not sure. He got really quiet and then pulled away."

"What'd you tell him?" Bert turned to look over his shoulder.

"That I was engaged."

"Ooh, no wonder he was hurt."

Hannah pulled back. "What? I was being honest."

"You broke the guy's heart."

"What? I did not. He married someone else. Obviously, he's moved on."

Bert snorted as he pulled off the freeway. "Um, okay."

Hannah huffed and folded her arms. What did Bert know, anyway? He wasn't a love genie. No matter what he said about himself. He didn't know their history. Logan was just fine. They'd both moved on. He just needed time like she always did. Yeah, Logan would be fine.

Hannah stared out the window as the shops passed by. But why didn't that thought make her feel any better? Her gaze landed on a boy standing in the middle of a fenced in area. He was surrounded by Christmas trees.

Her mom's bare living room entered Hannah's mind. Sitting up, she leaned forward. "Pull over."

CHAPTER ELEVEN

HANNAH

Bert slowed. "Here?" He nodded toward the trees.

"Yes."

Bert pulled into an empty spot and turned off the car.

"I'll be just a minute." Hannah opened the car door and got out. She waited until a truck passed by her, then ran across the road. The boy that stood next to the table eyed her. She smiled at him. "Hi."

He nodded. "Here for a tree?"

She glanced around. "What's the biggest one you have?"

His grin grew wider. "The Big Mama," he said as he started walking toward the back with his eyes as wide as saucers.

"The Big Mama?" she asked as she followed after him.

He weaved in and out of the trees. "It's an eight-footer. The biggest one I got." Suddenly, he stopped, and Hannah almost ran right into him. She followed his tilted face upwards to see the largest Christmas tree she'd ever seen. It was everything she'd been missing in her life. It was perfect.

"Sold," she whispered.

"Three hundred dollars," he said, extending his hand.

Hannah grabbed her purse and rifled around until she found her credit card. She tried to ignore the thought that this one tree was half her apartment's rent as he swiped it and handed it back. She squared her shoulders. The tree was worth it. She was going to have an amazing Christmas this year. She'd be sure of it.

"I'll net it up for you. Is that your car?" He nodded toward Bert.

"Yep."

"Give me five."

Hannah nodded as he made his way back to the tree. Once he disappeared, she walked across the road and met up with Bert.

"Get what you needed?" Bert asked as he leaned against the outside of the car.

"The Big Mama!" Hannah smiled at him.

A worried look flashed over Bert's face. "How big?"

The boy from the tree lot appeared, carrying the top of the tree with what looked like his dad following behind, carrying the trunk. The tree looked even larger horizontal.

Hannah smiled sheepishly over to Bert, whose eyes were wide.

"Seriously?" he asked.

Hannah nodded. "Please?"

Bert grumbled "You owe me," he said.

"Of course."

It took a good ten minutes of both men grunting and shoving to the get the tree on top of the car and tied down. Hannah grabbed a five from her purse and tipped the boy, who took it, then gleefully returned to the lot.

"Sure, you tip the boy." Bert gave her a semi-serious look.

"Hey, I'll tip you." Hannah started rifling around in her purse again.

Bert shook his head. "I'm teasing."

They both got into the car and headed back to Hannah's house. The tip of the tree ran the length of the windshield and ended on the middle of the hood. Bert drove slowly, which allowed Hannah to see all the quizzical looks people were casting their direction. All she could do was smile. Getting ready for Christmas did help with all her knotted up feelings.

Once they got to her mom's house, Bert pulled into the driveway. When he turned off the engine, they both got out. Circling around the car, they glanced at each other.

"We can do this," Hannah said, but it came out more like a question.

Bert raised an eyebrow. "You and me?" A deep rumbling laugh erupted from his lips. "Um, I don't think so. And I'm not killing my back for some Christmas cheer."

Hannah headed in his direction. "Come on. We can do this!" This time, it came out more confident.

Bert's gaze ran up and down Hannah. "Um, I think this tree weighs about the same as you do."

Hannah growled. "I'm stronger than I look."

"Is that your tree?" Piper's excited voice piped up from behind Hannah.

"Piper!" Hannah said as she turned around. "Yes. Isn't it exciting?"

Piper got off her bike and took off her helmet. Her eyes were wide as she scanned the tree. "It's ginormous!"

"Mr. Bert over here doesn't think that I can help him carry it. He's talking crazy, right?" She flexed her arms toward Piper.

Piper eyed her. "Um, no."

Hannah shot her a hurt look. "What? I can't believe neither of you believe in me."

"Honey, it's a matter of reality, not belief," Bert said.

"Piper!" Mrs. Blake called from the front stoop of her house.

"Grandma, come look at the tree Miss Hannah bought." Piper waved her over.

A few seconds ticked by before Mrs. Blake came into view. "What did I tell you about bothering the neighbors?" she said as she approached Piper.

"It's awesome, huh," Piper said, nodding toward the tree. It was obvious she was good at ignoring her grandma.

Mrs. Blake glanced at the car. "Well, that has to be the biggest tree I've ever seen."

"It's called The Big Mama," Hannah said, leaning over.

"Ah. Appropriate name. How are you going to get it down?" Mrs. Blake turned to look at Hannah.

"Me," Hannah said.

Mrs. Blake raised her eyebrows.

Agh, another person who doubted her strength. It was starting to feel personal.

A beeping sound filled the air. Bert reached into his pocket and pulled out his phone. "Hello?"

Hannah watched him as his expression fell.

"I'll be there," he said, then pulled the phone from his face and shoved it back into his pocket. "Gotta go, girlie. I'll get it down, but you'll have to get it in the house."

"Bert—"

"Emergency. I gotta go." Bert waved his hand in Hannah's direction as he headed toward the ropes that tied the tree to the car. As he loosened each knot, the tip of the tree snapped up. Then the back of the tree was freed. After a few shoves, it was rolled from the roof and flopped onto the grass.

"Sorry to leave you like this, but I gotta go," Bert said as he sidestepped the tree and got into the driver's seat. After he started the car, he pulled down the driveway.

Hannah stood there with her lips open. Now what was she supposed to do? Turning to Mrs. Blake and Piper, she smiled.

"Oh, no. I just had my hip replaced. I can't lift that." Mrs. Blake backed away from it as if it had radioactive material.

Hannah's gaze fell to Piper, who grinned up at her.

"I can help," she said.

Hannah smiled. She liked her enthusiasm. "All right. Let's do this."

Mrs. Blake turned. "Let me know when you get it into the house. I think I have some extra decorations in the attic."

They both nodded as Piper grabbed the tip of the tree, and Hannah grabbed the trunk. They lifted it, but it didn't budge. The middle of the tree stayed fixed on the ground.

Hannah set her side down. "This is harder than I thought."

LOGAN

Logan sat at the kitchen table, reading the magazine that was in front of him. Well, reading might be a stretch. He was more staring at the pictures and words, but the only thing floating through his mind was Hannah. She was engaged. Apparently, Samson and Hannah were more involved than he thought.

Reaching out, he grabbed a nearby roll and took a bite. It didn't matter anymore. She'd moved on, which meant he needed to as well.

The back door opened, and his mom came in. She glanced over to him.

"How's it going, honey?" she asked as she peered out the kitchen window.

Logan just grunted, but his mom didn't take notice. Instead, she was staring at something outside.

"What are you looking at, Mom?" Logan asked.

"Piper's helping Hannah lift a tree."

He stood, shaking his head. What did she just say? He made his way over to his mom and followed her gaze. Sure enough, Hannah and Piper were circling a giant tied up Christmas tree.

"They're going to lift that?"

"Apparently."

He studied them. Part of him wanted to go out and help. It was almost painful to watch them attempt to lift it. The other part of him wanted to stay in his house forever. Here, Hannah couldn't hurt him. She had a fiancé—she should call him for help.

Turning, he caught sight of his mom, who was watching him.

"What?" he shrugged.

"You know what, Logan Blake. I didn't raise you to watch people struggle and not help."

"But, Mom..." Man, he sounded like a whiny teenager.

"No buts. Go help Hannah."

He flexed his jaw. "But—"

She stuck her finger out. "Now."

Grumbling, Logan obeyed. He rolled his shoulders once he got outside. He needed to protect himself from Hannah.

"Need help?" he asked as he approached.

Hannah turned. "I think we have this. Right, Piper?"

Piper scrunched up her nose. "No. We don't. We need help."

Hannah shot Piper a defeated look. "What? We were doing so well."

"We haven't even moved it an inch."

Hannah laughed, but it slowly petered off when she turned her gaze to Logan.

Not waiting for her to come up with another excuse as to why he shouldn't help her, he grabbed the tree around the middle and lifted it.

Hannah opened her lips, but he shot her a glance. He could help her. It didn't hurt anyone.

"Thanks," she said, her voice barely a whisper.

He nodded as he passed by her and walked up the front stoop. He waited as she pulled out her key and opened the door. It took a little finagling, but he got past the wreath and the door frame with very few branch casualties.

Setting the tree down on its trunk, he glanced around.

"Where do you want this?" he asked as Hannah stepped inside.

Her eyes widened as they scanned the room. "I...um, didn't realize just how big it was."

Logan smiled. Such a Hannah thing to do. "Maybe over there?" He nodded toward a corner of the longest wall where the front window drapes were pulled open.

Hannah nodded. "Yeah, that'd be good."

Logan picked up the tree and brought it over. He propped it up on the trunk and glanced over to Hannah. "Stand?" he asked.

Her face paled. "I don't have one."

"Really?" Who buys a tree without a stand?

"Relax, I've got one," his mom called from the front door as she stepped into the room with her arms full of decorations.

Hannah's shoulders relaxed. "Thanks, Mrs. Blake." She ran to grab the boxes that were piled high in front of Logan's mom.

Logan could now see his mom's face. She smiled at Hannah and walked over to the tree where she set the rest of the boxes down. "You're lucky Mr. Blake doesn't let me throw anything away. These are the decorations from his mom."

Hannah grabbed the tree stand and brought it over to Logan. "I will definitely thank him."

Logan heaved the tree up, and Hannah slid the stand underneath. Once it was secured, he stepped back and tried not to laugh. The tip of the tree was bent a good five inches.

"This is massive, Hanny B." He turned to smile at her.

There was a look in her eyes as she met his gaze. It was familiarity and happiness all wrapped up into one.

Suddenly, she burst out laughing. "What was I thinking?" she said, clutching her sides. The sound of her happiness caused Logan to laugh.

Piper walked in and glanced at the two of them, then over to her grandma. "What are they laughing about?"

His mom turned to the tree. "Maybe the tree is too big?" She shrugged. "I'm not really sure. I think they've gone crazy."

Hannah reached up and dabbed her eyes. "Sorry. It's been a long day, and I bought a tree that doesn't fit."

Piper glanced at each of them again. "I don't get it."

Hannah shot Logan a look, then shook her head. "It's okay. I'm just a little loopy right now."

Logan nodded. "It's adult stuff, Pip."

From the look on Piper's face, she'd already lost interest. "Okay." Then she walked over to the boxes and pulled one open. Reaching inside, she emerged with an ornament. "These are old," she said with her nose wrinkled.

Hannah walked over. "Let me see." Reaching inside, she pulled out a Bugs Bunny ornament. "These are fun!"

"What are they?" Piper asked as she pulled a few more out.

"These are cartoons from when I was younger."

Piper fiddled with the metal hooks that dangled from one them. "Weird. Can I help decorate?"

Hannah glanced at her, then over to Logan.

Logan stepped forward. "Pip, it's rude to ask. We don't want to intrude on Miss Hannah."

Hannah shook her head. "You know what? I'd love the company." Pulling out her phone, she swiped it on. Soon soft Christmas songs filled the room.

Hannah and Piper opened all the boxes and began pulling lights and tinsel out. Logan fought it, but his heart surged. Seeing Hannah and his daughter work together was just a bit too much. He needed to be careful, or he'd lose his heart. Again.

CHAPTER TWELVE

HANNAH

We wish you a Merry Christmas filled the living room as Hannah started untangling the lights. Piper was next to her, wrapping the string into a circle as it became available.

"What was Christmas like at your house?" Piper asked, glancing over to Hannah.

She smiled. She really liked Piper. There was something about her that put Hannah at ease. "Quiet. I was an only child, and my parents divorced when I was young. I had to pick where I spent Christmas."

Piper chewed her lip. "I hope my mom comes this year." Then she leaned in. "I even asked Santa to bring her."

Glancing over to Logan, Hannah took in his forlorn expression as he studied Piper. Her heart went out to them. It must be hard for Piper to be away from her mom. It was nice that she had Logan and Mrs. Blake. They seemed to care a lot for her.

"I'm sure your mom wants to see you, too." She smiled at Piper.

Piper gave her a small smile.

"At least you have family here to celebrate the holidays with." Hannah picked at a particularly stubborn knot.

"Eh," Piper said.

"Hey," Logan said as he threw a bow in her direction.

Piper shrugged. "What? I see you all the time."

"Done!" Hannah said as she freed the last knot. "Now, Piper, let me tell you the best way to decorate." Standing, she ushered Piper over to the tree. "It goes, lights, tinsel, then ornaments."

"Hey, now. She's a Blake. We need to teach her the Blake way. Tinsel, ornaments, then lights."

Hannah stared at Logan. Was he serious? "Again? We're going to have this fight again?" She shook her head. "That way needs to die with the Blakes'. Piper, my way is the best way."

Logan walked over and fluffed one side of the tree. "Want to make it interesting?"

"Like a bet?"

"More like a wager."

Hannah's lips turned up. This was the Logan she remembered. Always trying to make things interesting. "Okay. What do you have in mind?"

"I'll take this half of the tree, and you take that half. We'll both have Piper help us, and she can decide who's right."

Piper's eyes lit up.

"Okay. If I win, what do I get?" Hannah asked.

Logan drummed his chin as he glanced around. "If you win, I'll make dinner."

Hannah's eyes widened. Logan made a mean lobster tail. "Okay. And if you win, I'll make dinner."

A snort filled the air. "Nah, that would be a punishment for me."

Hannah reached out and smacked his arm. "Hey, now, I'm not that bad of a cook."

Logan turned to face Piper. He put his hands to his neck as he rolled his eyes. "She's terrible." He nodded to Piper. "Remember when you tried to make bread last year with just flour and water?"

Piper giggled. "Yeah. It tasted like baked glue."

"Exactly. Bleh." He stuck his finger in his mouth. "That's Hannah's cooking all the time."

Hannah grabbed a string of tinsel and whipped him with it. But it was too flimsy and it just sank to the ground. "I'm not that bad. I've gotten better."

Logan nodded toward her like he believed her, then turned to Piper and shook his head.

"Okay, mister wager man. I'll take that bet." She stuck out her hand and tried to muster a confident look.

Logan shook it with laughter dancing in his gaze. "It's set." He squeezed her hand as he smiled at her. Butterflies flitted around in her stomach. She pulled her hand away. Inside, she took a mental note to never touch Logan Blake again. There was too much complication there.

Piper rocked back and forth on her feet. "This is going to be so fun!"

They got started. With only half the tree to decorate, Hannah had to get creative with the lights. Finally, she decided that a zigzag pattern was the best way. She had Piper plug in the strand to make sure it worked. The room filled with multi-colored lights as they twinkled on the floor.

"Pretty!" Piper exclaimed as she grabbed the strand. Hannah instructed her how to make sure the lights got on every branch.

Once they were finished, Logan enlisted Piper's help in flinging the tinsel onto the tree. He'd found a bag of icicle tinsel and claimed it as his. With each strand that floated to the ground, Hannah tried not to cringe. She wasn't sure how her mom would feel about this.

But the squeals of laughter that emerged from Piper's lips soon pushed away all that worry. Logan had her up on his shoulders so she could reach the top. Every so often, one would float down and land on Logan's head. Once they were finished, Logan looked like he was wearing a silver wig.

"Piper," he exclaimed as he hunched his back. "I'm the Christmas monster." He growled and headed after her.

She screamed and dipped behind the couch. He chased her, and she squealed as she rushed over to Hannah. "Save me, Miss Hannah." She crouched in the corner, shielding her face.

Feeling the energy those two were giving off, Hannah grabbed a few bows and stuck them to her head. "I'm the Christmas knight. I will protect you!" She grabbed a nearby icicle ornament and stuck it toward Logan.

He growled and lunged. "Perfect. I eat Christmas knights for breakfast." He pawed the ground as he readied his stance. Suddenly, he raced across the room.

Hannah couldn't help it, she screamed as she bolted away from him. He growled and chased after her. After three laps around the room, Hannah peeled off into the dining room. She glanced around for Piper. But she was no help. She'd taken that opportunity to climb on top of the piano to protect herself.

"Be careful, he tickles!" she called from her perch.

"Piper!" Hannah exclaimed. "You're supposed to help me." She narrowed her eyes at the approaching Logan.

"You're on your own," Piper called after her as she raced into the kitchen.

Two hands engulfed her waist and pulled her toward him. Her left foot caught on the right one, and she went tumbling down. Before she could hit the floor, Logan pulled her hard so that she landed on top of him. His eyes danced with excitement as he stared up at her. Her hair had been loosened from its bun and ringlets fell around them.

His breath was labored as his face grew serious. She became very aware of the warmth of his hands at her waist and the feel of his body underneath hers. They were no longer kids. Logan was a man. Her heart sped up as she met his gaze. Silently, she cursed herself for looking. There was a desire there that she'd never seen before.

"You okay?" he asked. His voice was deep with emotion.

Hannah pinched her lips and nodded. She was too afraid of what she might sound like if she spoke.

He reached up and pushed a curl behind her ear. "Can I tell you something?"

She nodded.

He brought his head up from the floor so he was inches from her ear. "You're crushing my guy parts," he whispered.

Heat flushed her body as she rolled off of him. He sat up, bringing a knee up and draping an arm across it. He glanced over to her. In the light of the kitchen, she swore she saw him blush.

"Sorry about that," she said. "I guess we got a bit carried away."

He smiled and nodded. "Yeah."

Piper emerged in the door frame. Hannah was thankful they'd gotten off each other. She didn't want to have to explain that.

Hannah stood and grabbed a glass from the counter and filled up the water. Logan sat cross-legged on the floor.

"You guys ready?" Piper asked, glancing around the kitchen.

Logan nodded. "Let's finish this up so I can beat Hannah once and for all."

Hannah turned and flicked some water at him. "We'll see about that."

He grinned at her, and her stomach turned to mush. Well, shoot. What was she going to do now?

They made their way back into the living room. Hannah enlisted Piper's help in putting up the tinsel as Logan sifted through the ornaments to pick the ones he wanted to use. Hannah kept a watchful eye to make sure he didn't pick the best ones.

Finally, both sides of the tree were decorated. Piper and Hannah stepped back while Logan plugged the lights in. It was a hodgepodge tree. But it made Hannah smile. The ornaments hung crookedly on the branches. In fact, they only went up about halfway. It was pretty apparent where Piper could reach and where she couldn't.

The lights on Logan's side seemed to be desperately clinging to the tips of the branches. She huffed. Obviously, her way was the better way. But in all its imperfections, it was theirs. They had made it together.

Glancing to the side, she saw Logan staring at her. Her cheeks flushed as her spine tingled.

"Grandma's tree is prettier," Piper said, breaking up their moment.

Logan glanced down at Piper. "What do you mean?"

She waved to the tree. "It's a mess!"

Logan reached down and grabbed her. Bringing her up, he hugged her tight. "But we did this!"

Piper giggled as he set her down. "Next time, we're asking Grandma. Both of your ways stink."

Hannah smiled. "It might be the tools we had to decorate with."

Piper turned and studied Logan, then Hannah. "No. You don't have Grandma's touch."

Hannah glanced at Logan and burst out laughing. "Maybe she's right."

Logan feigned a hurt expression. "I'm a Christmas tree-decorating master." He wiggled his eyebrows as he turned back to the tree. "You know what this needs? Our very own, hand-picked ornament." He glanced over to Hannah. "What do you say? We pack up and head to the store to pick one out. Then we can grab food for dinner as well."

Hannah couldn't help but smile at him. That idea sounded great. If she was honest with herself, she didn't want them to go. Who knew when her mom would be home, and she didn't want to spend the rest of the night alone. "That sounds amazing," she said.

LOGAN

Once they were piled into the cab of his truck, Logan pulled out of the driveway. Hannah sat in the passenger seat with Piper sandwiched between them. As much as he fought it, his heart soared. This was what having a family was like. He never wanted it to end.

Piper leaned forward and turned up the Christmas song on the radio. Soon, she and Hannah were singing along with *The Twelve Days of Christmas*. It was one of those songs that got faster as it went along.

They giggled as they tried to keep up. Logan enjoyed listening to them.

When the song was over, Logan turned the music down.

"That was... interesting," he said as he glanced in their direction.

Piper smiled. "I'm getting faster." Her toothy grin made his stomach flip. After what she'd said earlier about wanting her mom around for Christmas, Logan couldn't help but feel like a total failure as a dad. All he wanted was for his little girl to be happy. He'd find Charity and make her come if he had to.

"Yeah, Pip. You're getting better." He reached out and tousled her hair.

He turned off the freeway a few exits before they had to. He wanted to run past the old Victorian homes that ran down Johnson street. They always had amazing decorations.

"You going down Johnson?" Hannah asked as she turned her gaze to him.

He nodded. "Yep." He stopped at a light and waited.

"You know, my family used to own a house on Johnson street."

Piper grabbed a book from behind them and started flipping through the pages. Their conversation was most likely boring her.

"Really? I didn't know that," Logan said as the light turned green.

"Yeah. It's the Cobbler mansion. Apparently, my great-great uncle inherited and was supposed to live there, but decided he'd rather have the money."

Logan flipped on his blinker and turned down Johnson. Giant houses, most three stories high, ran the length of the street. The lights glinted and glittered as they framed the windows and roofs. Dancing Santas and reindeer dotted the lawns. Every yard had a lit-up nativity scene. Logan wondered if this street was visible in space.

Piper abandoned her book to look out the window. They all oohed and aahed at the festivities. Three neighbor kids were parked in front of a house under a sign that said, Hot Chocolate $2.

Logan pulled over and bought three cups. He paid with a twenty, but refused any change. He liked supporting kids who wanted to be entrepreneurs. Their eyes widened as he turned, which made him smile. It made his day to see them so excited.

When he got into the truck, they started back down the street. As they neared the Cobbler mansion, Hannah sucked in her breath.

"No way!" she exclaimed as she sat up straighter.

"What?" Logan peered through the windshield.

"It's for sale." She rolled down her window and waved toward the realtor sign in front of the house. "That's crazy."

Logan eyed the Victorian-style home. It was massive and its yard even larger. He glanced over at Hannah. "Your family owned this?"

She nodded. "I would love to buy it back." Then she laughed. "But it's probably millions of dollars. Where would I get that kind of money?"

The cab grew quiet. Logan glanced over at the house again. He had the money. A thought brewed in his mind. What if—

"It's a dream that will never come true. Maybe I'll call the realtor and schedule a showing." She smiled over to him. "I could pass as a rich man's wife, right?"

Logan studied her, then nodded. "Of course." He stopped at the light, then turned right. They got back onto the freeway and headed toward Shopping Co. The music filled the air as they rode in silence. He was thankful for the time to think. He needed to digest his idea.

CHAPTER THIRTEEN

LOGAN

It didn't take long before they pulled into the parking lot of the Shopping Co. and Logan turned off the engine. Hannah and Piper didn't waste any time climbing from the truck. Logan followed behind them. He watched as Piper linked arms with Hannah. He cleared his throat as he watched them interact. He doubted this night could get any more perfect.

As he walked past Mr. Cornwell, who was getting into his truck, Logan noticed a strange look on the man's face. Lifting up his hand to wave, Mr. Cornwell nodded as he continued studying him.

Then, Betsy Gordon stopped to wave at him. Her tie-dyed hair stuck in every direction. "Hey, Logan," she said, wiggling her fingers at him.

He nodded in her direction. "Betsy."

She giggled and flashed him another smile.

This was getting weird. He did live in a small town so knew most everyone, but they'd never been this friendly before.

Logan shook his head. It must be the holiday season that had everyone in a good mood.

When they got into the entrance of the store, Hannah grabbed a cart, and Piper hopped onto the side. As they meandered through the aisles, Logan tried to ignore the inquisitive looks the other store goers were giving him. What was happening?

They stopped in front of the ornaments. Piper jumped off the cart and started inspecting them. She grabbed a princess castle, a dog, and a crown from the wall. She stood next to Hannah while they deliberated about which one to get. Logan was fine taking a backseat to this. He'd end up picking the wrong one, anyway.

George, a little boy who went to school with Piper, came rushing into the aisle. He stared at an ornament in the shape of a baseball bat. He picked it up and held it gently between his fingers.

"George Allen Gunderson, get back here right now," a woman's voice scolded as she rounded the corner, almost running straight into Logan. She harrumphed as she stared at him. "Logan," she said as she nodded toward him.

"Mrs. Gunderson," he replied.

"Put that ornament down. We need to leave." She stomped over to George and pulled at the ornament he had tried to hide behind his back.

"But, Mom!" he whined as he glanced around in desperation. "Why does Piper get to buy one?"

Mrs. Gunderson glanced over to where Piper and Hannah were now looking at them. "Well, her family is rich. He can afford these things. Not like us—those who have to *work* for a living." Her tone had turned icy as she shot a glance in Logan's direction.

Logan stared at her. How did she know? His lips parted as

he tried to think of something to say to her. Something to rewind time so that Hannah hadn't heard. So that no one knew.

"Let's go," she said, grabbing the ornament and throwing it into a nearby pile. She pinched George's arm and dragged him from the aisle.

Logan glanced over to where Piper and Hannah stood. Piper had gone back to the ornaments, but Hannah had a look on her face that said she wasn't going to leave it alone.

She left Piper's side and headed in Logan's direction.

He readied himself for her questions.

"What was with Mrs. Gunderson? She seems really upset with you."

Logan shrugged, hoping he appeared as if he didn't care.

"And what was that about your family being rich and not working?" Hannah peered up at him.

He sighed and glanced over, tapping a nearby Santa ornament with his finger. "I'm... um..." He wasn't ready for this. This was his dad's money. Not his.

"Logan..." Hannah's voice sounded just like his mother's.

His shoulders slumped. "My dad left me a substantial amount of money when he passed."

Hannah's eyes widened. "Substantial? Meaning what?"

He shrugged and continued fiddling with the ornament. "I'm like a"—he dropped his voice—"billionaire."

Hannah leaned forward as if to try to catch what he just said. "A mill..." she started, eyeing him.

"Billionaire."

She took a step back. "So I did hear you right."

Logan's cheeks burned as he glanced over to her. "But it's my dad's money, not mine."

Hannah's lips fluttered as she glanced up and down the aisle. "Logan, this is insane. You know that, right? I mean, how can you not be running up and down the store? A billionaire?"

She made a choking sound as if that word had caught in her throat.

Frustration and pain boiled up inside of him. This is why he didn't want people to know that he had money. They didn't understand the pain associated with it. He was only rich because his dad was dead. The man he'd longed to have in his life since he was a small boy, trying to play baseball by himself. It didn't work. There was no one to throw the ball.

The urge to protect himself surged through his body. "I'm... I'm going to go get stuff for dinner. Watch Piper for me," he mumbled as he darted from the ornaments.

"Logan—"

But his hasty retreat cut her off. Right now, he needed to be alone. She, of all people, should understand that.

HANNAH

Hannah's ears rang as she watched Logan practically sprint from the aisle. Her brain stumbled as she tried to think of something to say. Anything. But, the only word she could think of in huge, neon letters was: *billionaire*.

How does one go from destitute to loaded in a blink of an eye at twenty-five?

As she brought her attention back to reality, she glanced over to Piper, who was dangling an ornament in her face.

"I think this is the one I want," she said, smiling her toothless grin up at Hannah. The ornament was in the shape of a princess castle.

"That's the one?" Hannah cleared her throat.

Piper nodded. "Yep."

Hannah grabbed it and placed it into the shopping cart. "Okay, let's go help pick out the food for dinner."

She led Piper down the aisle.

"Can we get Swiss rolls?" Piper asked.

"Sure."

"Great. I love Swiss rolls. At my mom's house, I always left them out for Santa."

"Swiss rolls, huh? No cookies?"

Piper glanced at her with a twinkle in her eye. "I figure, Santa will have his fill of cookies. If I leave him something he hasn't had, he might be so happy that he leaves me the biggest present of all."

Hannah's mind went to Logan and his earlier confession. With an uncle that rich, Santa was about to get really generous. "Makes sense."

They headed down the meat aisle and caught sight of Logan. He was standing in front of the cooler, staring a bit too hard at the packaged meats in front of him. Hannah's heart broke. She hadn't meant to upset him like that. Obviously, his dad's money was a sensitive subject. She really stuck her foot into her mouth this time.

They pushed the cart up to him.

Hannah leaned over to Piper. "Hey, Swiss rolls are down that aisle there. Wanna go grab them?"

Piper's face lit up. "Go get them? Alone?" She did a little jump where she stood.

"Come right back," Logan's voice sounded behind her.

Piper nodded and raced away. Hannah wondered if she wanted to get away before Logan decided against letting her go alone.

Taking a deep breath, she turned to see Logan had returned his attention back to the meat.

"Having a hard time?" she asked as she stepped up next to him.

He rested his hands on the edge of the cooler as he leaned

forward. She could see the tension that had built up in his shoulders. It had to be hard, losing a parent like that.

"I'm sorry," she said as she reached out and rested her hand next to his. From the corner of her eye, she saw Logan turn his gaze toward her fingers.

"It's just hard. I didn't know my dad and when I finally met him, he was dying. I had only a few years to make up for all the years he was gone." His shoulders slumped further as if he were recalling the memories.

"That's hard."

"And now I have this money, and I don't feel right about spending it. My mom's pressuring me to invest in all of her friend's ideas, but I don't know what to do. I want to make my dad proud." His voice grew fainter.

"I'm sure he's proud of you." Hannah leaned closer and nudged him with her shoulder.

He glanced back at her. There was a depth to his gaze. Raw and exposed emotions. She found herself swimming in the dark blue of his eyes. Her heart beat so loud, she could hear it in her ears. His warm hand engulfed hers as they stood there, locked in each other's gaze.

"Logan, I..." She didn't know what to say or how to say it, but there was something deep down inside of her that was fighting to come out.

"I got it!" Piper's voice broke the silence of their interaction. A thud sounded.

As if Hannah had been burned, she jumped back and glanced over to Piper's look of triumph. A box of Swiss rolls sat in the middle of the shopping cart.

"Great," she said, smiling.

Piper looked curiously at the two of them. "What were you doing?"

Hannah waved toward the cooler. "We're just picking out some meat."

Piper groaned. "Still? Ya'll are moving slower than molasses." She made her way over to the meat and pointed to one. "I want that."

A giant lobster tail sat on a Styrofoam tray. Logan reached out. "You gonna eat it this time?"

Piper smiled. "Yep."

"Lobster it is," he said as he dropped it into the cart right alongside Piper's Santa-bribing Swiss rolls.

After all the ingredients were gathered, they checked out, and headed back to Logan's truck. Hannah let Piper get in first. While she waited, she helped Logan load the groceries into the back.

As he shut the tailgate, he turned to her.

"Thanks," he said.

She glanced over to him. "For what?"

"Thanks for listening to me. And letting me have my little pity party. I know it can be hard to believe that this sudden status could be hard. I mean, I'm set for life, but it's hard"—his voice cracked as he swallowed—"this money came at a price."

Hannah reached up, wrapped her arms around his shoulders, and hugged him. Even after everything they'd been through, they were still friends. "I'm sorry," she whispered.

He hesitated, then wrapped his arms around her waist and drew her closer. There was a familiarity to his touch. She took in the scent of his cologne. It still hadn't changed. It had a woodsy smell to it.

"I've missed you," he said, his voice muffled by her hair.

The loud piercing sound of his truck's horn filled the night air. Groaning, Logan stepped back. "Piper," he grumbled as he glanced down at Hannah.

"Sorry," he said, nodding toward the cab.

Hannah giggled. "It's fine. She's probably hungry."

He nodded but then grew serious. "Thanks for that. I know after everything we've gone through..." His voice trailed off as he eyed her.

Hannah's stomach tightened at the mention of their past. But she just brushed it off. Best not to think about that right now. "We'll always be friends."

He hesitated, then nodded. "Friends."

Hannah made her way to the passenger door as Logan walked toward the driver's side. Once they were in and buckled, Logan started the truck and peeled out of the parking lot.

Piper had turned up the volume to *I saw Mommy Kissing Santa Claus* and was singing to the words at top volume.

Hannah glanced out the window toward the twinkling lights that adorned all the houses. Her emotions were muddled and confusing her. The anger and betrayal she'd felt on prom night when she realized that Logan had abandoned her weren't as strong as they'd been before. It was as if being around him was slowly etching away her angry feelings.

She swallowed as Logan's voice broke into her thoughts. He was begging Piper to sing a bit quieter. Piper, of course, took this as a challenge and sang even louder.

As Hannah glanced over to Logan, a thought settled in her mind. Perhaps, just perhaps, she might be forgiving the billionaire.

CHAPTER FOURTEEN

HANNAH

When they got to Hannah's house, Logan grabbed all the groceries and headed into the kitchen. Hannah tried to follow, but Logan pushed her out, stating he had dinner covered.

Walking into the living room, Hannah glanced over to Piper, who was curled up on the couch. Well, she had about a half hour to kill. She made her way over to Piper. "Wanna see my dolls?" she asked.

Piper shot up like a rocket. "Yes!"

Hannah smiled and walked over to the staircase. "Wait here. I'll go get them." She climbed the steps two at a time.

Once in her room, she made her way over to her closet and pulled it open. Up on the top shelf were two boxes. Pulling them down, she blew the dust off of them. Her mother wouldn't let her take them to her father's house. Hannah wondered if it had something to do with the fact she left her mother the way she did.

Pushing away the angry feelings she got every time she

thought about their relationship, she sighed. No sense in dwelling on that right now. She tucked the dolls under her arm and headed back downstairs. Piper was sitting cross-legged on the carpet with her eyes wide.

Hannah joined her. Setting the boxes down on the floor, she pulled off the tops. Piper squealed as she gently took out Hannah's Samantha doll. Her fingers brushed the doll's dark hair.

"She's beautiful," Piper whispered.

Ah, Hannah had found the secret to getting Piper to talk at a normal decibel. Just bring out her dolls.

After getting out her Truly doll, they started playing. They each brushed their doll's hair. Hannah had a few extra outfits and they took turns changing their clothes. Piper chatted on and on about which doll she wanted and which outfit would go perfectly.

Hannah smiled as she listened. Then Piper grew serious as she recounted a story about Reagan, a girl from her class last year, who'd made fun of her because she loved the dolls so much.

"That's not right," Hannah said after Piper confessed she'd pushed Reagan on the playground.

Piper stuck out her tongue. "Well, she deserved it."

Movement by the doorframe drew her attention over to it. Standing with his shoulder leaning against the wall was Logan. He was watching them with a smile on his lips. Hannah met his gaze, and he raised his eyebrows.

"Having fun, ladies?"

Piper nodded. "Miss Hannah has the best dolls."

"Miss Hannah does. Miss Hannah used to try and make me play dolls with her." Logan pushed off the wall and made his way over. Reaching down, he grabbed one of the shoes that were scattered across the floor.

"When Santa brings me a doll for Christmas, you'll be playing with me as well," Piper said matter-of-factly.

"Oh, really?"

Piper nodded and continued brushing Samantha's hair.

"Any chance you ladies are hungry?"

Piper dropped the brush to her side. "Can Samantha come?"

Logan laughed. "Sure."

Soon, Hannah, Piper, Logan, Samantha, and Truly were all sitting at the table. The smells that wafted from the dishes caused Hannah's stomach to grumble.

After their plates were loaded up with butter-basted lobster tails and parsnip puree, they dug in. Hannah couldn't believe how good all the food tasted. No one spoke as they ate.

Once her plate was emptied, she glanced over at Logan, who was watching her. Reaching up, she rubbed her face. Did she have something there?

"What?" she asked.

He shrugged. "It was nice to see you playing with Piper."

Hannah glanced over to Piper, who was talking to Samantha. Apparently, Samantha needed to clean her plate or she wasn't going to get dessert. Hannah wondered how many times that little girl had heard the same thing.

"She's a sweetheart." Hannah couldn't help it. She had a soft spot for the girl. Then her mom's warning voice broke into her thoughts. She always did that. Fall for every person she met. But that little girl's red hair and contagious smile had wormed its way into her heart.

"May I be excused to go to the bathroom?" Piper asked, and Logan nodded.

The room grew quiet.

"I just wish her mom felt the same," Logan said as he placed his fork onto his plate.

"She's not around a lot?"

Logan shook his head. "She's decided that dancing is more important than her daughter." His jaw flexed as his gaze fell on the chair that Piper had vacated.

Hannah nodded. She knew what that felt like. Her mother's job always took precedence over her. She was here to visit and yet, her mom was at the hospital. Christmas was in two days. After that, Hannah was headed to her dad's. This was the time to mend their relationship, yet her mom was nowhere to be found.

"If I were her mom, I'd never let her go." She smiled at Logan. She meant it.

Logan glanced over at her. There was a look in his eye that she couldn't quite place. "Really?" he asked.

Hannah smiled. "You bet. Any woman who picks her job over her daughter doesn't deserve her."

Logan cleared his throat and broke their gaze as Piper made her way into the room. "Pip, you done?" He nodded toward her plate.

"Yep," she said. "Can I watch a movie?"

Hannah wiped her lips with her napkin and set it next to her plate. "How about *Home Alone*? That was my favorite growing up."

Piper scrunched up her nose. "Never seen it."

Hannah's mouth dropped open. "What? Okay, we're watching it. Right now." Pushing from the table, she waved toward Logan. "Come on."

Logan glanced around the table. "I should probably clean up."

Hannah shook her head. "Nonsense. We can do that later."

Logan looked skeptical but then nodded. "Okay."

"Movie's under the TV. I'll pop some popcorn," she said.

Logan nodded as he followed Piper from the room.

The kitchen air filled with the smell of buttery popcorn as Hannah pulled the bag from the microwave and shook it. After grabbing a bowl and dumping the popcorn into it, she grabbed a few waters and made her way out to the living room.

Piper was sitting between each of the dolls, which put Logan right smack dab in the middle of the couch. Hannah inspected the small space to the left of him. Realizing how close they'd be sitting next to each other, Hannah wondered if she should say something about the stack of dishes in the kitchen.

But before she could complain, Piper spoke up. "Come on, Miss Hannah. Samantha and Truly are ready."

Logan shrugged and motioned toward the seat next to him. "No backing out now."

Hannah's face heated. How had he guessed? She made her way over and sat down. Just as she sank into the couch, her body tipped toward him. Blast him and his heavy body. Wiggling, she tried to move closer to the armrest. It didn't work.

Piper started the movie, but Hannah just couldn't get comfortable.

"You okay?" Logan asked after the previews were finished.

Hannah glanced over to him. "Yes. Why?"

He smiled as he grabbed a handful of popcorn. "You're wiggling worse than a trout pulled from the water."

Hannah sighed. "You're just so heavy."

He glanced at her with a hurt look plastered on his face. "It's just holiday weight."

She glared at him. "You've always been heavier than me."

"Hey, don't be hating on me and my muscles." He reached out and flexed his bicep.

"Shhh..." Piper shot them a pointed look.

Hannah raised her finger to her lips and nodded. They all turned their attention back to the TV. Soon, Hannah accepted how close Logan was to her. In fact, she was enjoying it. They fit together. She'd never noticed that before.

Her eyes grew heavy, so she leaned her head against his shoulder. She felt him tense, but she didn't move. If she had to get comfortable with them touching, so should he.

Ten minutes later, Logan tapped her shoulder.

"Look," he whispered as he pointed toward Piper. She was asleep with each doll wrapped up in her arms. She looked like an angel.

"Aw," Hannah said, turning to look at Logan.

He was inches from her face. Inches from her lips. He met her gaze as his face grew serious.

"Hannah..." He reached out and brushed her hair away from her face.

It was too much. Hannah pushed back and stood. "We should probably clean up. My mom will freak if she sees the house like this."

Logan's smile faded. "Okay."

They stood and Logan headed into the kitchen while Hannah made her way to the dining room. Here, it was safe. Here, she wouldn't accidentally kiss Logan Blake. She knew all too well the heartbreak that would follow.

LOGAN

Logan grabbed a plate and flipped the water on. The caked-on food angered him. Grabbing a scrub brush, he zoned in on it. There was no way this food particle would win.

Once it was obliterated, he moved on to the next dish. Destroying dried-on food wasn't helping to relieve the ache that had taken up residence in his chest. Why was it when he tried to get close to Hannah, she just pushed him away?

The water burned his fingers as he rinsed the dish. He

groaned. Not from the shocking temperature, but from the way his heart soared when he saw her sitting on the floor playing with Piper. Every moment he spent with Hannah, she was rapidly becoming the girl he wanted to spend all his moments with.

Desperate for a distraction, Logan reached over and flipped on the radio. Christmas music filled the air as Logan continued working on the dishes. When the commercials started, Logan flipped to a different channel. *When a Man Loves a Woman* caused him to stop. It was the song they'd danced to at prom.

Hannah walked into the kitchen and stopped. The dishes in her hands dropped a few inches as she took in the music. When her gaze reached him, his heart hurt. There was so much pain and frustration built up in them. No longer waiting for her permission, he covered the distance between them in two steps.

Taking the dishes from her hands, he placed them on the counter. Then, he reached out and pulled her close.

"Logan..."

"Hannah, I'm sorry," he said as he grasped her hand and began to lead her around the kitchen. "It was my fault. All of it. I'd made a stupid decision and it hurt you."

She was no longer fighting the dance, but he could tell there was something holding her back.

"I know you're engaged, but—"

"I'm not engaged," she whispered.

His heart soared from her confession. "What? But you said—"

"I lied. Well, my boyfriend proposed, but I didn't know what to say. I've run home to avoid him." She bit her lip as she turned her gaze up to him.

He tightened his grip on her. "Hannah, why would you lie about that?"

She focused on something to her left. "I wanted to protect myself."

Ouch. Logan slowed as he bent down to catch her gaze. "You will never have to protect yourself from me again. I won't ever hurt you. You mean too much."

Hannah glanced back at him. "I don't know if I can trust you."

Logan stopped dancing. Reaching down, he grasped both sides of her face. "Hannah, I will always protect you." His gaze slipped down to her lips. The memory of them against his flooded his mind.

It seemed as if that memory was as fresh on Hannah's mind as it was on his. Her features softened as he leaned closer. When she didn't pull away, he closed the gap. The warmth of her lips filled his every sense and all the feeling of pain and frustration he'd been carrying since that fateful prom night rushed from his body. Suddenly, he knew exactly where he wanted to be. Right here.

Deepening the kiss, he wrapped his arms around her waist. Her body fit against his like a puzzle piece. Her fingers made their way up to his hair. Desperate for some air, he pulled back for a moment before he leaned back in, this time, teasing her lips with his. She giggled as she returned the feather light kisses.

"Hannah," he breathed as he pulled back and brushed a kiss on the tip of her nose.

"Logan."

Pulling back farther, Logan glanced down toward Hannah. Since when did she sound just like his mom?

"Logan," the voice repeated. "Look who's here."

His mind cleared as he glanced toward the back door. Toward his mom. Toward Charity.

"Charity?"

Hannah pushed away as she looked sheepishly toward his mom and his ex. "I'm sorry."

Logan glanced toward Charity. "What are you doing here?"

Sputtering from the doorframe drew all of their attention toward it. Piper stood there with a sleepy look, and she was staring at her mom. Her eyes widened as a smile spread across her lips. "Mommy!"

CHAPTER FIFTEEN

HANNAH

Hannah stood there. She felt as if her body weighed a million pounds. Did Piper just say *mommy?*

Glancing over at Logan, she noticed he was watching her. If Charity was Piper's mom, that meant that Logan was her dad, not Bobby.

"You're Piper's dad?" Hannah asked.

Logan looked at her with a pained expression on his face. "I tried to explain to you—"

Piper didn't seem to notice the tension that was thick enough to cut. She raced over to Charity and wrapped her in a hug. "You're back. I asked Santa for you to come, and look!" She grasped both sides of Charity's face and planted a kiss on her cheek.

For a moment, it looked as if Charity was cringing. As quickly as it came, it disappeared. "I missed you, too, Pip." She grabbed Piper's arms and pushed her away.

"Hey, Piper, I gotta dishwasher that needs to be unloaded," Mrs. Blake offered.

"On it." Then she paused. "You're not going anywhere. Right?" she asked, turning to her mom.

"I'm not going anywhere," Charity said as she stepped away from Mrs. Blake and up to Logan, grabbing his hand.

Hannah's stomach summersaulted, and she wanted to throw up. All she wanted to do right now was run upstairs and lock herself in her room. What was Bert talking about? Christmas was not a magical time. At least, not for her.

Once Mrs. Blake had shepherded the bouncing Piper from the house, the kitchen grew silent.

"So. Who are you?" Charity asked as her icy gaze landed on Hannah.

"This is Hannah. Remember her?" Logan asked.

Charity's gaze ran up and down Hannah's body. Suddenly, she felt extremely exposed. Wrapping her arms around her chest, she took a step back. Five more steps and she'd be out of the room.

"Oh, Hannah," she said, dragging out every syllable in her name. "The girl you took to prom."

Logan glanced down at Charity. For a split second it seemed as if he glared at her, but it just might have been Hannah's desire for him to detest Charity. Why had she allowed herself to care for him again? The feelings that swarmed her mind that night at prom returned. This time, with a vengeance.

"And my best friend," Logan added.

"Was," Charity said, raising her perfectly manicured finger toward him. "You can't have a best friend other than your wife."

Logan took a step back. "We're divorced. You said you couldn't stand me anymore. Said I held you back."

Charity's high-pitched, squeaky laugh filled the air. "I was out of my mind." She turned and rested her hand on his chest. "I've changed. I want to be a family again."

Hannah needed to get out of there. "This seems like a personal conversation. I'm just gonna..." She pointed toward the door and then turned, praying no one would ask her to stay.

"Honey, this is your house. We'll just go," Charity said.

Hannah stopped. Charity's voice caused prickles to race up and down her spine. But, she did have a point. When she turned back around, Charity had Logan's hand in hers and was pulling him toward the door.

"Hannah, I..." He pulled free from Charity's grasp and took a step toward her.

"Logan, come on. Let's go back over and spend some time with our *daughter*." She glanced over to Hannah and narrowed her eyes.

Logan's gaze never left Hannah's face. "Please, let me explain."

Hannah cursed the tears that threatened to spill. This was not how she wanted any of this to go. She needed some time alone to think. "You should go," she whispered, trying to ignore the pain that rushed over Logan's face.

"But, I need to tell you." He reached out with his fingers inches from her arm.

"I'm not interested." The words fought against the lump in her throat. Truth was, she didn't want to hear either way. If he wanted to be with his ex, that would break her heart. But, if he wanted to be with her, that would break Piper's heart. Hannah wasn't sure which situation would hurt more.

Charity made her way back over to Logan and wrapped her hand around his arm. "See? She's not interested. You know who is? Your wife and daughter." She tugged him in the direction of the door. "Let's not keep our princess waiting."

Hannah's heart dropped to the floor as Logan took one

more pleading look at her, then turned. Five seconds later, the kitchen fell silent as Charity shut the door.

A sob escaped Hannah's lips as she let the tears flow. Broken-hearted, she made her way over to the kitchen table and collapsed on a pulled-out chair. Pushing the dish in front of her to the side, she rested her folded arms on the tabletop. Her shoulders shook as the tears streamed down her face.

The back door opened and, for a moment, she allowed the feeling of excitement to rush though her as she pulled her head up. Was it Logan coming back?

But her mom's exhausted body filled the door frame. She was studying the mail in front of her. As she looked up, a surprised expression crossed her face. Her gaze ran the length of the kitchen before it landed on Hannah's face. Then her expression turned sour.

"What happened?" she asked.

Another sob escaped Hannah's lips. "Logan was here—"

"Logan? Logan Blake?" Her mother let out an exasperated sigh. "Hannah, what did we talk about? No visitors."

Hannah raised her eyebrows. "It was Logan Blake," she said as she wiped the moisture that had accumulated under her nose.

Her mom massaged her temples. "Hannah, it doesn't matter. You broke my trust. Again."

"Mom, I'm sorry. I...just..." She studied her mother's pinched lips. All she wanted was for her mom to listen to her. To try to understand what she was going through. Instead, she'd disappointed her mom. Again.

Instead of justifying, Hannah's shoulders slumped as she studied the crumbs on the table. "I'm sorry. I should have respected your wishes. I'll clean up."

Her mom sighed. "Thank you." Walking across the floor,

she stepped out of the kitchen and into the living room. "Hannah!"

Hannah cringed. That didn't sound good. She stood, even though every molecule of her body told her stay put. "What's wrong, Mom?"

She walked into the living room to see her mom standing there, staring at the Christmas tree. "What did you do?" She made her way toward the tree, then stopped. "And your dolls?" She reached down and picked them up. "I worked so hard to keep them perfect." She pulled out the rubber band Piper had used to hold Samantha's hair back.

"Mom, these are dolls. My dolls."

Her mom placed them back into the boxes. "If you play with them, they will get ruined."

Hannah wanted to scream. She wanted to shake her mom and tell her it was because of her obsessive need to have everything perfect that she was breaking her daughter's heart. But, instead, all she wanted to do was run away.

"I have to make a call." Hannah turned and headed toward the stairs. Her mother had made her way over to the Christmas tree and was picking the icicle tinsel from it.

Once in her room, Hannah sat down on her bed and stared at her hands. The all too familiar feelings of pain rushed through her body. Everything had seemed so perfect and now? It was as if she were living the past all over again. She grabbed her phone and did the only logical thing her brain could process right now. She called Samson.

LOGAN

Logan's body felt numbed as he sat on his couch, staring at Charity. She was here. Sitting next to him. Holding his hand. He blinked as he shook his head. What was she doing here?

"And that's when I decided that I'd been a fool, so came back to find you." She turned and smiled at him. When he didn't respond, she leaned closer. "Logan? Did you hear what I said?"

Feeling stupid, he cleared his throat. "Sorry. Just trying to digest this information. It's been weeks, months even, since I've heard from you." He scrubbed his face with his hand and stood. He needed to get away from her. "Since Piper has heard from you," he said with his voice low as he leaned in.

Thankfully, Piper was so tired after helping his mom that she agreed—with little protest—when he suggested she head to bed. Right now, he needed to speak freely with Charity. Something he couldn't do with Piper's little ears listening.

The lights on the Christmas tree twinkled as he turned and studied them. His thoughts turned to Hannah and the tree they'd decorated together. Their tree. Try as he might, he couldn't get the look she had on her face out of his mind. She must feel so confused right now.

"So, what do you think?" Charity's question broke into his thoughts.

"What?"

"About us trying again?"

Logan sighed and stared out into the darkness. "I don't know, Charity. You've been gone so long, what am I supposed to say?"

She stood and walked over to him. Wrapping her arms around his waist, she pulled herself close. "Say yes." She looked up at him.

The feeling of pain and sadness that always followed her seeped from her embrace and settled in Logan's stomach. He needed to distance himself from the whirlwind that was Charity Monson. "No, Charity. We're done."

Even though she looked as if she wanted to say something

further, Charity stepped back. "Well, it's Christmastime. You never know." She made her way back over to the couch. "I think it'd be best if I stay here with Piper." She glanced over to Logan.

Acid rose up in his throat. "I'm not—"

"Come on, Logan. It's Christmas."

She kept saying that like it meant something. What happened to the last five Christmases where she basically abandoned her daughter? Didn't those matter?

He clenched his jaw. As much as he wanted to point that out, he knew it might unhinge Charity and cause her to run again. Piper would be so upset if she woke up to her mom gone. He couldn't disappoint his daughter like that.

"Fine."

Charity smiled. "Good."

He waved her toward the stairs that led to the basement. "You can stay in Tim's room."

Charity raised her eyebrow. "Down there?"

Logan nodded. "If not, there's a nice motel about ten minutes out. I can call you a cab."

She chewed her lip, then smiled. "Nope. Basement's fine."

Once she was at the bottom of the stairs, she turned and looked up at him. "See you in the morning."

"Yep." Then he turned and headed up the stairs to his room where he was secretly hoping that Hannah was sitting outside on the roof. He desperately wanted to talk to her.

He shut his door and headed over to the window. One glance and his heart sank. She was nowhere to be seen. Her bedroom light was on, but her drapes were shut tight.

He contemplated grabbing an item and chucking it to her window to get her attention but then thought against it. He was sure Miss Kathy wouldn't appreciate a broken window.

Instead, he flopped down on his bed. Glancing up at the popcorn ceiling, he brought his fingers to his mouth.

The memory of Hannah's lips rushed back to him. His heart pounded as he thought about her body against his. He rolled to his side. Then, Charity had to go and mess things up again. Was this his fate?

A soft knock broke him from his frustration. He sat up. "Come in."

The door opened, and Piper peered into the room from the crack in the door. "Daddy?"

"Hey, Pip." She pushed the door open farther and, in the faint glow of his side lamp, he saw her tear-stained face. "What's wrong?"

She sobbed as she sprinted to his bed and climbed up. "Is Mommy still here?"

He wrapped her up into his arms and pulled her next to him. She laid her head on his shoulder and sobbed again.

"Sh, sh," he whispered as he rubbed her back and rocked her. "She's here. She's downstairs sleeping in Uncle Tim's old room."

Piper pulled back. "So she's not mad at me?"

He wiped a strand of hair from her face. "Why would she be mad at you?"

She sobbed again and buried her face into his shoulder. He could feel the moisture from her tears seep into his shirt. "Because it was my fault," she whispered.

His heart broke from the pain this little girl carried. Pulling her back, he looked into her eyes. "What's your fault?"

"You and Mommy fighting all the time. If only I'd been a better girl, Mommy would have stayed."

He wrapped her back up into his arms and held her tight. If he could, he'd take all her pain away. "It's not your fault. Really," he said with his voice deep with emotion.

"So you won't make Mommy go away?" She pulled back and stared at him, wiping some snot away with the back of her hand. He grabbed a Kleenex from on his nightstand and motioned for her to use it.

"Of course, I won't make Mommy go away." He smiled.

"And you'll think about us becoming a family again?"

His stomach flipped. She'd heard. "How do you know about that?"

Her face reddened. Her lips hung open as if she were trying to come up with an answer. Finally, her shoulders slumped. "I listened."

Pulling her back, he looked into her eyes. "I promise you, you little sneaky girl, that I will do what's best for the two of us. If that means making things work with Mommy, then I will."

She stuck out her pinky. "Promise?"

Logan met her gesture. "I promise."

She snuggled into his chest and within three minutes, was fast asleep. When he returned to his room after laying her down, he climbed into bed. He was too tired to think anymore today. Right now, he needed sleep. In the morning, he'd deal with his mess of a life.

CHAPTER SIXTEEN

LOGAN

Voices from the kitchen carried up the stairs and into Logan's room. He rolled onto his back and stared up at the ceiling. He winced as his mother's decibel showed her frustration. She was upset with someone.

He scrubbed his face. What was he going to do? Charity was here, and he'd promised Piper he would try and make it work. But at this moment, all he could think about was Hannah. How she'd played with Piper. How she made him feel. And last, but certainly not least, how her lips felt against his.

Groaning, he threw his covers off and headed into the bathroom. He needed a cold shower.

Once he was out and dressed, he opened his door and strained to hear the voices downstairs. They were still at an unsafe volume so shut his door again. He decided to head over to the window. Glancing out, his heart stopped. Hannah was sitting on her roof with her knees pulled up to her chest, staring out into the distance.

He glanced at his bed and flexed his hands. No. He couldn't go out there. What would he say? What would she say? He glanced back at Hannah, then back to his bed. After about twenty times of starting to walk toward the window only to detour to his desk, his bookshelf, and then his dresser, he took a deep breath.

Get a grip.

Forcing a smile, he pulled open the window and stepped out onto the shingles.

He glanced in Hannah's direction. She hadn't noticed him. Instead, she kept her gaze toward the horizon. Briefly, she brought her mug to her lips and took a sip, then placed it back down. The sun's morning rays illuminated her face. She was beautiful.

"Hey," he offered, nodding in her direction.

Startled, she jumped and turned. When her expression fell, Logan thought his heart would break. No longer was there laughter and excitement in her eyes. Now, only pain and regret clung to her gaze.

"Hey," she said, turning back to the horizon.

Determined to get her to talk to him beyond these ridiculous pleasantries, he settled down on the roof. "It's a beautiful morning, huh? Hard to believe that Christmas is tomorrow."

Hannah nodded and sipped her tea again.

"Any big plans?" He rested his elbows on his knees.

Hannah glanced over at him. "After tomorrow night, I'll be heading to my dad's to celebrate Christmas morning."

"Oh."

She gave him a small smile as she twirled a leaf between her fingers. "How are things with Charity?"

Oh, right. That. "Okay. She's staying here to visit with Piper." He narrowed his eyes. "And only Piper."

Her gaze found its way back to his, and he held it. The only sound that surrounded them was the light trill of a bird off in the distance. He was desperate to read her. Had he ruined everything? Again?

"So—"

"Hannah—"

They both stopped and looked at each other. Hannah pinched her lips together.

"You go," he said, waving toward her.

"No. You go first," Hannah said, nodding toward him.

"I insist."

Hannah paused as she eyed him. "So, you had a baby with Charity."

He nodded. "Yeah."

"While we were in school?"

He nodded again. "I made a mistake. It was a one night mistake. Before, you know..." He wanted to tell her it was before he realized he had feelings for her. Before that fateful prom kiss.

"But Piper's great." Her gaze wandered over to the dark windows on the side of his house.

"Yes. She's one of the best things that has ever happened to me." He intensified his gaze. Hannah was the other. How could he help her see that? She had to know that he cared for her. Deeply.

Hannah studied him before she dropped her gaze to the roof and traced her fingers along the edge of one of the shingles.

"I found out that Charity was pregnant on prom night," he confessed.

Hannah's gaze whipped to his face. "What?"

"I left that night because I'd just found out about the pregnancy. She called to say she was taken to the hospital because of bleeding. I needed to be there for her. I should have never left you like that, but I didn't know how you'd react..." He let those words linger in the air as he watched her face, hoping she'd give him a reaction or something. Anything for him to go off of.

"You could have told me." Her voice was hoarse with emotion.

"I didn't know how."

Their gaze met again, and Logan could see all the hurt and betrayal she'd felt for so many years. And he'd caused it. He wanted to rush over there and hold her in his arms. He wanted to protect her, but all he seemed to be doing was breaking her heart.

"Prom night... Last night... You have to know—they meant something to me," he said, testing the waters.

Hannah chewed her lip. "But that's the problem with the past. It's the past. Here. Now. This is your future. Charity and Piper—they're your future."

"But, Hannah—"

"Stop. You have a daughter you have to think about. If you and Charity can make it work, you should do it." A smile teased her lips. "Piper's such a good kid. She deserves that chance."

"But, Hannah, I can't just..." His heart was breaking with each word she spoke. He wanted to tell her. She had to know. He loved her. He'd loved her since he pulled her hair in kindergarten.

"No. Let's leave what we had in the past. I'll cherish it. But you and I will never work. We should have taken that hint from the cosmos from the beginning." Her smile turned into a sad one. "I'm happy for you. Really." She wrapped her arms around her legs as she rested her chin on top of her knees.

Logan swallowed. This was not what he wanted, but he couldn't force her to love him if she wouldn't. He couldn't force her to be with him if that's not what she wanted. "You're great. You know that?"

She shrugged. "Yeah."

Her phone rang, and she picked it up. Looking up at Logan, she covered the phone with her hand. "I should take this." She stood and made her way toward her open window. Once inside, she disappeared from his sight.

Not wanting to sit on the roof and pine after Hannah, Logan stood and made his way back into his room. Shutting the window broke his heart. For some reason, as the window thudded into the place, all he could think about was the fact he was shutting it on Hannah.

He rolled his shoulders. There was one thought he needed to get used to and used to now. They were officially over. Hannah wanted nothing to do with him, and he had to accept that. It was time to see if Charity really was different. Even though his stomach twisted at the very thought of starting over with her.

HANNAH

"You're here? You've landed?" Hannah tried to keep her gaze from making its way back over to the window. Her heart still ached from the conversation with Logan, but her mind reassured her that this was the right thing to do. Piper deserved to have both parents, and she wouldn't be the person to stand in the way.

"I'm here, babe. Excited to see you," Samson's New York accent drawled over her speaker.

"Great. I'll call you a cab. I know a guy."

"Sure. Tell him I'll meet him outside of baggage claim."

"Perfect..." She hesitated. Why was she hesitating? "I love you."

"Love you, too."

As she hung up the phone, she stared at the picture of Samson. His messy hair and half smile no longer caused butterflies to erupt in her stomach. All she could think about was Logan.

Groaning, she flung the phone across her bed and it slipped off the edge. Flopping down, face first, onto her comforter, Hannah groaned. Since when had her life become such a muddled mess? She should have stayed in Ohio. North Carolina was the wrong move. Even if it was Christmas.

Bert. She needed to call Bert. After a few minutes of searching around under her dusty bed, she emerged triumphant. Hitting his number on the speed dial, she brought the phone up to her cheek.

"Whatcha need, girlie?" he drawled.

"First, how are things with you? What happened yesterday? Is everything okay?"

His deep laugh rumbled through the speaker. "Yeah. Everything's okay. My wife cut her finger pretty bad opening the cat's dinner. Had to take her to the doctor. She got five stitches."

Hannah cringed. She hated slicing her finger on cans. She was no stranger to that. "I'm happy to hear everything's okay."

"Yeah. Her pride's hurt a bit, but she'll mend up nicely." He paused. "So, did you need something?"

Hannah sighed. Oh yeah, that. "I need you to pick up my fiancé."

There was sputtering on the other side. "Your what?"

"My fiancé."

"How long has it been since we talked?"

Hannah picked at some lint on her bed. "Yesterday."

"What happened to that boy next door?"

Hannah groaned. She did *not* want to talk about Logan.

"He's getting back together with his ex."

There was silence. "Bummer."

Hannah forced a smile even though he couldn't see it. "It's okay. I'm over it. Besides, I'm marrying Samson."

There was a soft chuckle from Bert. "And I need to get him?"

"Yep."

"Airport?"

"Yep."

"On my way."

"Thanks."

He hung up, so she put the phone down on her bed. She wanted to get up. She wanted to go downstairs and clean up the mess she'd made with Logan last night. But going down there meant facing her memories and she wasn't sure if she was ready to do that just yet.

A text chimed on her phone, and Hannah picked it up.

Bachelorette party tonight, maid of honor! With a few too many emojis after.

Hannah stared at it. Was she serious?

But, I haven't planned anything.

No problem. Tricia had it planned. She's emailing you the itinerary right now.

Another chime sounded. Sure enough, **Bachelorette Party Details** showed up in her inbox. Big block letters and all.

Hannah sighed. This was not what she wanted to do right now. Hiding in her bed under her covers was how she was planning on spending her evening.

Got it. I'll look it over

Another chime. *Can't wait! Tomorrow I'm a married lady.*

Before Hannah could answer, there was a pretentious knock on her door. Ugh, even her mom's knock sent chills down her spine.

"Yeah?"

"I was called into the hospital," her mom called through the door.

Hannah sighed. Of course. "Okay, Mom."

Silence. Hannah gnawed on a nail. She was looking forward to Christmas morning when she'd be at her dad's house and not here.

"Can I come in?"

Her mom's voice caused Hannah to jump. She thought she'd gone. "Um, sure?"

Her door opened, and her mother stood there with a strained look on her face. After a few seconds of awkward silence, Hannah waved to her mom. "You can actually come in."

Her mom took a wary step into her room and crossed her arms. "I had some time to think about how I acted last night, and I wanted to say I'm sorry."

Hannah's jaw almost fell off. Was her mom *apologizing*? "Um, okay."

"You were just trying to get into the holiday spirit, I understand that now. It's just that I need things to be a specific way." Her gaze shifted to Hannah's. "I don't do well with change."

Hannah's heart broke. She never wanted this kind of relationship with her mom. She loved her. If she was honest with herself, she wanted to be closer. "I know, Mom."

A tense smile spread across her mom's lips. "I was thinking that we could order some Chinese and watch *Jane Eyre* tonight."

"BBC version?"

Her mom nodded as if there really was no other choice. And there wasn't. Not in this family, at least. "Of course."

"Sure," Hannah said. She actually felt excited about this. Then Sandy's texts came back to her. "Wait, no."

Her mom's face fell. "Okay."

"No, it's not that, Mom. I promised Sandy I'd be her maid of honor and her bachelorette party is tonight." Then Hannah raised her eyebrows. "You could come with me." Hannah would actually like another familiar face there.

Her mom sputtered. "Like, strippers? I'm not sure I could handle that."

Hannah's eyes widened. She hadn't thought about that. What had she gotten herself into? "Hang on." Scrolling through her phone, she located the email. Clicking it open, she read the instructions. Thankfully, there was no stripper planned. She smiled up at her mom. "No strippers. Just a few bars and a mini golf place."

Her mom winced. "Hopefully, mini golf first."

Hannah peered at her mom. "Does that mean you're coming?"

She hesitated, then nodded. "I'll come. Drew says I need to get out more."

Hannah raised her eyebrows at her mom, who instantly pinched her lips shut.

"Who's Drew?"

Her mom kept her lips tight as she shook her head.

"Mom... Who's Drew?"

Finally, her mom sighed. "He's a nurse from the hospital. We're sort of...dating."

Hannah smiled. "Mom! Hopefully, an older nurse?"

Her mom's face flushed. "Of course. He's my age."

"Good. I didn't want to have the cougar talk with you."

"Hannah Bell. I am not a cougar—whatever that means."

SECOND CHANCE WITH THE BILLIONAIRE 137

"It means, you like young guys."

Her mom's eyebrows flew up.

"But I know that's not you."

"Thank you."

Hannah pulled a pillow from her bed and hugged it. "So, why all the secrecy?"

Her mom brushed down her shirt. "I didn't want you to know until we were serious. I didn't want to confuse you."

"Mom, that's for little kids. I'm an adult. You can tell me about your boyfriends." Hannah tried not to wince. The word tasted strange on her tongue.

"Regardless, I like Drew, and I'd like for you to meet him."

"It's serious?"

For the first time in Hannah's lifetime, she saw her mother smile. It was a carefree, joyous kind of smile. "Yes."

Hannah returned it. "I'm happy for you, Mom." Then she paused. "Speaking of guys, I'm engaged."

Her mother's eyebrows flew up. "What? To whom?"

"His name is Samson. He's actually on his way here right now."

An uneasy look passed over her mom's face. Then she shook her head. "I'd be fine if he stayed here. Downstairs, of course."

Hannah was shocked. "Wow, Mom. Really? You'd be okay with that?"

She nodded. "Really."

"Thanks." Maybe this Drew guy was the key to her mom's issues. Now she was intrigued. "So, tonight then?"

"I'll see you tonight."

When her mom was gone, Hannah glanced out the window. For the first time this holiday season, she actually felt hopeful. Maybe Bert was right. Christmas was a magical time. Too bad it wasn't magical enough for her and Logan.

CHAPTER SEVENTEEN

LOGAN

Logan gave up hiding in his room and headed down the stairs. He braced himself as he slipped into the kitchen. The counter was a mess and the sink was heaped with dishes. Charity sat at one end of the dining room table with a disgruntled look while his mom fumed at the other end.

"Ladies," he said as he made his way over to the cupboard and grabbed a glass.

His mom appeared next to him. "Charity stayed the night?"

He glanced at her while he drank the water from his glass. "Not in my room," he said as he put it down on the counter.

His mom's cheeks flushed as she glanced toward the basement. "That explains why I found her in Bobby's room this morning."

Logan's stomach lurched. He'd told her to go to Tim's old room, not Bobby's. He glanced at his mom, who was fighting back tears.

"No one's been in there since..." A sob escaped her lips.

"Mom, I'm sorry. I should have gone down there with her." He reached out and wrapped his shaking mom into a hug. When Bobby died, his mom couldn't bring herself to move anything or change anything. Instead, his belongings sat untouched all these years. Piper wasn't even allowed into the room.

His mom nodded into his shoulder. "Just get her stuff out of there."

Logan nodded as she pushed away and left. Turning, he glanced at Charity. She raised her hands.

"I had no idea. How was I supposed to know that was your dead brother's room?" She pushed away from the table and grabbed her bowl.

"Geez, Char." He glanced around, hoping his mom was out of ear shot by now. "Have some compassion."

She paused, her shoulders tightening. "Your *mother* came into the room and screamed at me to get out." She pinched her lips as she stared pointedly at Logan.

"You have to understand. My mom's not dealing with this." A fire burned in his stomach as he studied Charity. How could she be so insensitive about this?

Silence engulfed the room as Charity stood there. He wondered what she was thinking. Experience told him that when her eyebrows were furrowed like that and her gaze whipped around the room, she was about to let him have it.

"Mommy! You stayed!" Piper exclaimed as she came racing into the room and up to Charity. They embraced, then Piper pulled away and studied her, then Logan. Her shoulders slumped.

"What's wrong, pumpkin?" Charity asked.

"Were you and Daddy fighting again?"

Disappointed in himself for letting his daughter see his frustration, he plastered a smile on his lips and bent down. "Mommy and I aren't fighting."

She glanced at him and then back to Charity. "Really?"

Charity nodded. "Really."

"Good, 'cause I've got fun things planned for today. I was thinking we could go to Merdoc's hill and go sledding!"

Charity glanced up to him. "Merdoc's hill? Don't we need snow?"

Logan shook his head. "It's a dry ski slope. The day before Christmas Eve, they let families come and sled."

Charity smiled at Piper. "Let's do it!"

Piper squealed and pushed away. "I'll grab my shoes."

Before Logan could say anything more, his phone rang. Glancing down, he almost groaned. It was Jimmy. Right now, he didn't feel like running errands again.

"Hello?"

"Hey, if it isn't my best man." Jimmy's voice boomed from the speaker.

"How's healing going?"

"Eh, I'll be good as new if these doctors will just leave me alone."

Logan chuckled. Jimmy was never going to slow down, He always lived on the side of danger. "You need something?" He reached into the cupboard and pulled out a granola bar.

"Just making sure everything is in order for my bachelor party tonight."

A chunk of granola flew to the back of Logan's throat. Crap. He'd forgotten about that. "Um, yeah. It's gonna be great."

Jimmy chuckled. "You didn't forget, did you?"

"Of course, not. Your bachelor party is going to be epic."

Charity's gaze flew to his face and she raised her eyebrows. Logan waved it away.

There was silence on the other end. "Can I ask you something?" Jimmy asked.

"Shoot."

"So, I've been hearing some chatter and it is insane, let me tell you. But..."

Logan squinted as he tried to think what exactly Jimmy might have heard about him. As realization settled in his chest, he chewed a bit harder on the remaining bar.

"Are you...like, rich now?"

Crumpling up his wrapper, he threw it into the garbage. "Something like that."

"I mean, I know you said you got some money when your dad died, but from the way these people are talking, it was like millions."

Yet again, his relationships were changing because of this money. "Hey, Jimmy. It's all true. But it's not something I want to talk about right now. Just know, I have your party planned and it's going to be great."

There was a whooping on Jimmy's side. "Now it will be!"

The line cut off on Jimmy's laughter. Logan looked down at his phone. Did that mean he now needed to spend a ton of money on this party? Was this what the rest of his life was going to be? People expecting him to use his money?

Scrolling through his contacts, he located Veronica's number. He'd hired her to plan Piper's birthday party last year. They'd gone on a few dates, but decided to end it and just be friends.

He slipped into the hall. He didn't need Charity to hear their conversation.

"Veronica's Parties and Events."

"Ronnie? It's Logan. I need a favor."

After five minutes of explaining and waiting for her to calm herself once he told her money wasn't an issue, Logan hung up and headed back into the kitchen.

"Who was that?"

Logan tucked his phone into his pocket. "Jimmy and Sandy are getting married tomorrow. I've gotta plan the bachelor party."

"Sandy's getting married?"

Logan nodded slowly as he studied her. "Yeah. Why?"

Charity shrugged as she slipped on her shoes. "Nothing. Just thinking it might be nice to go to her bachelorette party. We did know each other in school. And she's your friend."

Logan winced. "I'm not sure that's a good idea."

"Why?" He could detect a hurt tone in her voice.

"Well, I'm planning Jimmy's and I'm guessing Hannah's planning Sandy's."

"Hannah? The girl you were kissing last night?"

"Geez." Logan glanced around, thankful to see that Piper had bounded outside and was twirling in the yard. "It was one time."

Charity narrowed her eyes. "Good. 'Cause I'm here to make this work." She turned and headed outside.

Logan flexed his hands and followed after her. As they walked to his truck, a cab pulled up in Hannah's driveway. Logan squinted against the morning sun as a man with dark hair and olive-colored skin stepped out. Heat raced from his spine as he watched Hannah rush from her front door and barrel right into the guy's arms. They hugged and kissed, and Logan wanted to throw up.

"Wow. She moves on fast," Charity said, coming up from behind him.

Logan's frustration kept him from saying anything. All he could do was stare.

"Miss Hannah!" Piper shrieked as she bolted across the yard.

Startled, Hannah pulled from the guy and glanced around. When her gaze met Logan's, her face turned beet red and she stepped back. Good. Let her feel uncomfortable. He'd been on the receiving end of her kiss last night. He knew she felt more for him then she was letting on.

"Piper! Good to see you." Hannah reached out and hugged his bouncing daughter.

"Who's this?" Piper stared at the man.

Logan walked up behind her. "Piper, don't be rude."

Hannah smiled at her. "It's okay. This is my very good friend, Samson."

"Huh." She turned to Hannah. "Are you still coming to the carnival today? We're going to Merdoc's hill, then heading over there."

Hannah glanced over to Logan. "I'm not sure—"

"But you promised."

"Piper, if Miss Hannah can't, then that's okay."

Piper glanced at Logan, then back to Hannah. "But she promised."

Hannah studied Piper's face. "Okay. I'll be there."

"Yes!" Piper squealed as she wrapped her arms around Hannah's waist. "I can't wait for you to meet my friends."

Hannah patted her head. "I'm excited, too."

Logan studied the two of them as they embraced. His heart hurt watching them. He was trying to deny his feelings for Hannah, but when he saw her hugging his daughter, all of his resolve went flying out the window.

Piper was the first to break the embrace. "Okay. Let's go, Daddy," she said as she bounded over to the truck and got inside.

"You don't have to come," Logan said, daring heartbreak to meet her gaze.

"I know. I want to. It means a lot to Piper. I don't want to disappoint her. I could never hurt that little girl." Hannah's gaze zeroed in on Charity.

"Will you be coming?" Logan glanced over to Samson, who pushed his hair from his face.

"Sure. If Hannah's going, then I'm going." He reached out and slipped his arm around Hannah's waist and pulled her to him.

Logan wanted to throw up and punch the guy at the same time. He shook his head. He was a mess of emotions right now. He needed to get a grip.

"Great. Can't wait to see you there." He turned and glanced at Charity. "Come on. Let's go."

It took less than thirty seconds for him to cross the yard, yank open his door, and start his truck. Thankfully, Charity was just as fast. They peeled out of the driveway.

Logan tried to keep his gaze from making its way over to Samson and Hannah, who were walking up the sidewalk that led to her house. He tried to keep his heart from breaking as Samson leaned down and brushed his lips across her cheek.

But from the way his heart tightened at the thought of them together, Logan knew he was in too deep. He needed a distraction.

"So, tell me what you've done since we saw you last," he said, turning to Charity. She smiled and proved, yet again, that she was more than happy to talk about herself.

She chatted on about all the different acting jobs she'd taken. The disgusting apartment she had to live in. Not to mention her overbearing roommate. When Piper tried to join the conversation, Charity waved her away. Finally, Piper gave up and started counting the semis as they passed by.

Such a stark difference between watching this mother-daughter interaction and watching Hannah and Piper play with dolls. Hannah welcomed and invited; Charity ignored and shut out.

Logan glanced in the rearview mirror and smiled at his red-haired beauty. She giggled and pointed at the semis that passed them. When he turned his gaze back to the road, he pressed on his brake to stop at a red light.

Glancing to the left, he peered down Johnson street. The Victorian house they'd driven by last night looked just as stately in the morning sun as it did last night with all the twinkling Christmas decorations. An open house sign had been added to the front yard.

Logan flipped on his blinker. "Hang on. I need to check on something." When the light turned green, he pressed on the gas. Pulling the car up into the driveway, he turned it off.

"Logan. What are you doing?"

He glanced at Charity. "Wait here."

She huffed and folded her arms.

Logan chose to ignore her as he shut the door and walked across the lush green grass. It spanned the front yard and ran up to the brick walkway. He went up the front steps that led to a giant wraparound porch. The front door was open and voices could be heard in a far room.

He pushed the button on the handle of the storm door and opened it. Stepping inside, he took off his shoes. "Hello?" he called.

The voices stopped and a woman with black-rimmed glasses and a pressed suit appeared. "Well, hello," she said, giving him a warm smile.

He nodded as he tried not to stare at the huge entryway he now stood in. The chandelier above him twinkled in the sunlight that was making its way into the room from the window above the door. An ornate staircase was centered in front of him and went off in both directions. His stomach flipped from the expensive furnishings that adorned the room.

And he could actually afford something like this. It was all too strange.

"Are you interested in the house?" the woman asked as she clutched the folder she had tucked next to her body.

His first instinct was to call foul and leave. But he could do this. It was for Hannah. He swallowed. "How much?"

The woman's gaze swept over him, and for a moment, he felt vulnerable. It was as if she were trying to gauge the seriousness of his question. "One-point-nine million."

He swallowed. Never in his life had he heard that number before. He was a back roads, thrift store kind of guy. His mouth dried as he glanced around. "I'll take it."

Her laugh echoed off the walls and rattled his resolve. "Honey, do you have a bank note stating this is something you can afford?"

He glanced over to her. "Trust me, I don't need a bank to help me pay for this."

She pulled the folder from her body and shuffled some paper. "Well, I can't do anything until I have that note. Here's my contact information. Give me a call once you have it."

He reached into his back pocket and pulled out his wallet. Flipping it open, he removed his lawyer's business card. "Call my lawyer. I'm offering cash. I'd like to take care of this today."

She studied him as she reached out and took the card. "I will."

He nodded and turned. Once outside, he let out the breath he'd been holding. The weight that he'd been carrying around since his dad's death seemed to lighten. This was what his dad wanted him to do with the money. He intended it to be a blessing to Logan's life. He wanted Logan to be happy. And right now—all Logan knew was—making Hannah happy made him happy.

CHAPTER EIGHTEEN

HANNAH

Hannah tried not to watch Logan's truck drive by as she followed Samson up the walkway and into her mom's house.

"This is your mom's house?" Samson asked, eyeing the Christmas tree in the corner.

"Well, the furniture and everything else is my mom's. That"—she waved to the tipping tree—"is mine."

Samson smiled. "I love it. Just like I love you." He leaned over and kissed her on the nose.

Hannah tried to ignore the feelings that settled in her stomach. This wasn't Logan. The kisses weren't the same.

"Oh, before I forget. I brought this." He rifled around in his suitcase and emerged with the little black box that had caused her to find the first flight out of Ohio and hide in North Carolina. "Ready to wear it?"

Her cheeks heated, but she ignored the feelings of hesitation. "Sure."

He grinned and opened the box. Taking out the ring, he

motioned toward her left hand. She extended her fingers, and he slid the ring onto the fourth one.

She stared at it. It sparkled under the overhead lighting. It was beautiful. A princess cut diamond surrounded by a circle of smaller ones. But she couldn't ignore the nagging feeling in her gut that told her something was wrong.

When she glanced up, Samson was studying her.

"Everything okay?" he asked, pushing his hand through his hair.

Hannah nodded. "Yeah. It's beautiful."

He grabbed his suitcase. "Yeah. My assistant did a good job."

That was strange. "You didn't pick it out?"

Samson shook his head. "You know I don't do that kind of stuff. Jenny is much better at it." He glanced around. "So, where am I sleeping?"

Curling her fingers into her palm, she lowered her hand. He didn't pick out the ring? His assistant did? That was about as personal as having the butcher pick out your meat. Shaking it off, she smiled at Samson. That didn't matter. They were engaged. Who cared how they got there?

"Follow me," she said, waving her hand at him. He kept a few steps behind her as she led him down the stairs.

"Down here?" he asked, glancing around.

Hannah nodded. "Mom's rule."

He gave her a sly smile. "But rules are for breaking."

"Not this one." She shook her head. She was finally on the road to mending her relationship with her mom. There was no need to test its limits right now.

Samson plopped his suitcase on the cot Hannah had set up and unzipped it. "I'll shower and then you can show me where you grew up."

Hannah nodded and headed back up the stairs. Once in

the kitchen, she sat at the table and twirled the new accessory around her finger. Her thoughts turned to Logan and the kiss they'd shared yesterday. Her lips tingled from the memory. Shaking her head, she instantly felt stupid.

They'd slipped into a moment of insanity. That was what last night was. They'd both moved on from their high school feelings. She forced a smile. They were friends. That was all they could be.

LOGAN

Logan studied Charity as she stood at the top of the hill, glancing down at the blue mats that covered the hill in front of them. "Really?" she asked, nodding in their direction.

"It'll be fun," Logan said, smiling.

Flipping her hair over her shoulder, Charity gripped the sled.

"You'll do awesome, Mommy," Piper said.

She grumbled something under her breath, then plopped the sled down and sat on top of it. She shot Logan one last glare, then pushed off. The sled started off slow, but then picked up speed. Soon, she was screaming and careening into other sledders. Logan laughed.

Piper glanced over to him. "Mommy isn't having too much fun, is she?"

Logan shrugged. "It's good for Mommy to get out of her comfort zone once in a while."

Piper chewed her lip. "Who was that person with Miss Hannah earlier?"

"Samson?"

Piper nodded.

"I'm not sure, sweetie. Why?" He studied her. She looked worried.

"I hope he doesn't take Miss Hannah away."

Logan wrapped his arm around her shoulders. "You like her, huh?"

Piper smiled up at him. "She's my best friend."

His heart felt as if it would burst.

"I tell her my secrets."

Logan feigned a hurt expression. "I thought I'm your only secret keeper."

Piper giggled. "You're the daddy. The dragon slayer."

Grabbing Piper around the middle, he tipped her to the side and brought her up by his hip. "Dragon? Did you say dragon? Where?" Pretending he had a sword, he swept it in front of him. "I'll slay any dragon that threatens Princess Piper."

Her giggle had turned into a full laugh as she tried to wiggle from his grasp. "Daddy, put me down. There are no dragons right now."

He placed her down, then bowed on one knee. "Your highness."

She pretended to knight him. "To the brave Sir Daddy. You have been knighted."

He wrapped her into a hug. As he pulled back, he studied her. "You like Miss Hannah that much?"

Piper nodded. "I don't want her to go."

Reaching out, he swallowed as he ruffled her hair. He shared her sentiments.

They spent the next two hours riding sleds down the hill. After Charity's fifth tumble into the trees, she gave up and stated she'd be sitting at the cafe while they finished. Logan waved to her as she walked away. He was grateful to have this time alone with Piper.

They were both red-cheeked and sweating as they walked into the cafe around lunchtime. Charity was sitting at the counter, sipping on an ice water. Logan walked up and flagged down a waitress.

"Two waters, please."

"I want a lemonade," Piper said.

"A water and a lemonade," Logan corrected. The waitress smiled and disappeared.

"Are you guys done?" Charity asked after they settled in on the seats.

Logan glanced at Piper. "We done?"

"Yeah. I want to go home and get ready for the carnival."

Charity looked at Logan. "We're going to that?"

Logan nodded. "Yeah. I promised Audrey."

Charity glanced at her fingernails. "It's just not really my thing."

Logan tried to ignore the hurt look that passed over Piper's face. "Come on, Charity. Piper wants to introduce you to her friends."

Piper nodded and smiled at her mom.

"Pumpkin, Mom's really tired. Maybe next time. I'm not planning on going anywhere."

Logan's stomach lurched. He hated it when Charity made promises that she was clearly going to break. Then he'd be left to pick up the pieces. "Mommy shouldn't make promises she can't keep," he said through gritted teeth.

Charity shot him a look. "I can make that promise."

Logan narrowed his eyes. "It's okay to be practical."

"I am."

Anger surged through Logan, but he didn't want to fight in front of Piper. Reaching into his pocket, he pulled out a few quarters. "Why don't you go over to the arcade and play a few games. I'll order us food."

Piper squealed, grabbed the coins, and headed toward the

blinking game consoles. When she was out of earshot, Logan turned.

"Why did you do that?"

Charity fiddled with her straw. "Doing what?" She sighed.

"Promise our daughter that you were here to stay." He narrowed his eyes. "Especially when we both know you'll leave the minute you get bored."

She took a sip of her water. "Who says I'm going to get bored?"

"Experience."

"Well, you're wrong."

He scoffed as he picked up a menu and tried to make out the words written on it. "Believe me, Char. I wish I was. For Piper's sake, I wish I was."

A warm hand engulfed his fingers. He glanced up at Charity.

"I don't want to fight. I want to start up where we left off. Why can't we try again? Piper deserves to have her mom and dad together."

His chest constricted as he glanced over to Piper. She was cheering and pumping her fists in the air. As much as he wanted to fight it, he knew she was right. He was on a mission to make the women he cared about most happy. If being with Charity would make Piper happy—he'd do it.

He brought his thumb up and rubbed Charity's hand with it. "Okay."

Charity's eyes lit up. "Really?"

No. But he wasn't going to say that. "Yes."

A smile broke out over her lips. "Great."

The waitress came over, and Logan ordered lunch for him and Piper. Charity just waved her away, saying the water was just fine.

Fifteen minutes later, the food was dropped off at the table, and Logan motioned for Piper to come over. Silence filled the air as they started eating.

A phone rang.

Logan felt for it in his back pocket. It was his. Pulling it out, he hit the talk button. "Hello?"

"Mr. Blake?"

"Yes."

"This is Gertrude Templeton. I met you at the open house this morning?"

"Yes, Gertrude. What can I do for you?"

"Well, I contacted your financial advisor as you said..."

"And?"

"Well, the Kensingtons are willing to accept your full price offer if you are still in the market to buy."

A surge of excitement rushed through him. "So, it's mine?"

Gertrude hesitated. "Yes. It seems your finances are in order. They'd like to move forward with the sale as quickly as possible."

Logan grinned. "Great. Yes, I'll take it."

"We'll have the documents ready for you to sign after the holidays."

"Perfect."

Pulling the phone from his ear, he hit the end call button.

Two inquisitive gazes peered back at him.

"What was that?" Charity asked.

"It seems I bought a house," Logan said.

Charity sputtered on the water she was drinking. Reaching out, she grabbed a nearby napkin. "A house?"

Logan nodded as he picked up a French fry and began to chew. Wow. What a rush. Maybe this being rich thing wasn't so bad.

"Are we living there?" Piper asked. Then her face grew serious. "I don't want to leave Granny."

Logan's stomach flipped. "Oh, no, honey. It's not for us."

"What? Then who's it for?" Logan tried to ignore the accusatory look Charity was giving him.

"It's for a friend," he said.

Charity groaned. "Oh, no. Not Hannah."

Logan watched her. "What does it matter who it's for?"

Charity's shoulders stiffened. "I just think we should discuss things before making big purchases like that."

"What? It's my dad's money. Why should I have to run anything past you?"

Charity's eye's widened. Then she shook her head. "You're right. I'm sorry. It's your money—do with it what you want."

Logan took a bite from his hamburger. "Thanks, I will," he said through the buns and meat.

Charity folded her arms and sat back as if that wasn't what she wanted to hear. Logan brushed it off. It wasn't her money. She had to know that. Then a thought settled in his stomach. How did Charity know he had money? Had she heard? Was that why she was back?

"How did you know?"

She straightened as she glanced around at the families gathering at the other tables. "Know what?"

"About my dad's money."

She pulled the best innocent face. If this was her acting, then it was a wonder why she couldn't find a job. "What money? Dad? I don't know what you are talking about."

"Char, you just told me we need to discuss big purchases."

She flattened out her napkin on the table. "Well, it's true."

Logan glanced over to Piper, who was busy consuming her chicken fingers.

"If we're going to make this work, you need to be honest with me."

Charity studied him. Then she raised her hand. "Fine. I'll

admit it. I know about the money. But it wasn't until I'd already gotten here and had to go into the Gas and Stuff. Betty Jo told me." She folded her arms. "Were you going to tell me?"

Logan dipped his fry into his ketchup. "No. But that's because I wasn't going to tell anyone." Blast this living in a small town thing.

"Why not? This is a great thing." Charity leaned forward on her elbows. "We can finally do all those things we talked about when we were first married. Except more."

Logan's face heated as frustration boiled over. "Char, stop it. Now."

Her lips opened and he could tell she was fighting the urge to continue.

He shook his head as he raised his hand. "No more. It's my dad's money, and I'm not comfortable spending it."

She scoffed and leaned back. "Well, when?"

Seriously, she was fighting him about when he would be ready to start spending? "Let's just drop it."

"How much is a billion?" Piper asked as she peeked over to Logan.

"What?"

"While I was playing over at the games, Carter said his mom said you have a billion dollars. So, how much is a billion?"

Logan glanced over to Charity, whose eyes were wide.

"It's a lot of money, honey." He hoped she'd just drop the question.

Piper took a drink of her lemonade. "Okay, Daddy." She dunked her fry into some ketchup.

Glancing over at Charity, Logan inwardly groaned. From the look on Charity's face, she wasn't going to let this go as easily as Piper did. And he was pretty sure this was not a conversation he wanted to have.

CHAPTER NINETEEN

HANNAH

Hannah followed two overzealous moms dressed up as reindeer and a portly Santa Claus as she walked into the elementary school's gymnasium at a quarter to four. Bert had picked them up and dropped them off. His normally cheery disposition had changed as he eyed Samson. For some reason, that didn't sit right with Hannah. She wanted Bert to like Samson. As strange as that was to admit to herself.

"Wow," Samson said from behind her. "They really go all out."

As Hannah's gaze scanned the giant three-dimensional snowflakes that hung from the ceiling and the millions of twinkling lights that covered every inch of the walls, she nodded. "Yeah, they do."

I saw Mommy Kissing Santa Claus blared through the speakers that were set up on the far side of the gym. Tables lined the walls and were getting stocked with all sorts of goodies. Santa and the two reindeer had found the sleigh and were getting situated.

"Hannah, right?" Audrey's voice asked from behind her.

Hannah turned. "Right."

"Good to see you came," she said, eyeing Samson.

"This is my fiancé," Hannah said, waving toward Samson, who nodded.

Audrey's lips parted. "Fiancé?"

"Yeah."

"Wow—fast," she muttered as she glanced down at the clipboard she had tucked against her hip. "Well, Logan's not here yet, but the game you two will be running is in room 106."

Hannah followed her gesture toward the door. "We're in different rooms?"

Audrey called to someone behind Hannah, then turned her attention back. "Yeah. There's not enough room in here." She widened her eyes as if that was pretty obvious. "Do you know where Logan is?"

Hannah scanned the gym. "No. But he's out with Piper and Charity."

The clipboard tipped away from Audrey as she stared at Hannah. "Charity's back?"

Hannah's stomach churned. Why was this such a shock to everyone? What exactly had happened between Logan and Charity? "Yeah, she said something about wanting to work on their relationship." Audrey's jaw tightened. Perhaps it would be better to move the conversation forward. "I was hoping that I could run a booth with Samson. I'm sure Logan would like to be with Charity."

Audrey narrowed her eyes. "I'm sorry. I can't do that. If I allowed everyone to change their assignment because of an ex-wife or new fiancé, my life would be chaotic."

Hannah studied her. There was a hint of sarcasm in Audrey's voice. Why was she acting like this?

"What I do need help with is stocking the refreshments." She eyed Samson. "Think you can do that?"

Samson glanced over to Hannah and shrugged. "Does that mean I have to be around the kids?"

"Um, no. Not necessarily."

"Then I'm game. Never really like hanging with tiny adults." He leaned toward Hannah and lowered his voice. "Never been too fond of kids. Thank goodness this is the only time we'd need to do this."

Hannah stared at him. Was he serious? "What?"

"Excellent. Well, let's get you a hair net, and I'll introduce you to Blanca—she's the refreshment coordinator," Audrey said as she ushered Samson away.

Hannah watched him. She was trying to digest what he had just said. He didn't like other people's kids— she knew that already. But she'd always assumed he'd want their kids. How did she miss out on asking him how he felt? She chewed her lip as she made her way out of the gym and started scanning the hallways, looking for room 106.

When she got into the room, bags of supplies were dumped on the floor. A piece of paper was tacked to the wall. That was it. She sighed as she grabbed the instructions and studied them. They needed to decorate three of the cardboard boxes to look like stockings. They would be what the kids threw the coal into.

There was also a bag of ratty clothes that she and Logan needed to dress up in. They were to represent the naughty kids that didn't get presents. As she pulled out the tattered shirt and pants, she couldn't help but scoff. Who came up with this game?

Just as she dumped the supplies out of the bags, a voice carried into the room. Logan's voice.

"Stay in the gym if you're not going to hang out with me here," he said. His voice got louder, and Hannah contemplated running and hiding. She couldn't face the emotions that erupted inside of her every time she saw him.

From the corner of her eye, she saw him pause in the door frame. Her heart galloped as she felt his gaze on her. It took all her willpower not to turn and meet his gaze.

"You beat me here," Logan said, smiling at Hannah as he walked into the room.

"Hey, Logan," Hannah said, praying her voice would come out normal. "Yeah. I was hoping that Audrey might switch us, but she said she couldn't."

Logan was silent. Hannah turned and looked at him. His face had turned stony. She'd said the wrong thing.

"I mean, I thought you might want to spend more time with Charity," she stammered, trying to redeem herself.

He nodded and headed over to the decorations. "Yeah. I get it. No need to explain."

"Logan, I didn't mean..." She reached out, hoping to draw his attention back to her.

His hand reached out and grabbed her fingers. Turing her hand over, he studied the ring on her fourth finger. "So, it's official, huh?" he said, his voice low.

Hannah chewed her cheek. "Yes." She couldn't help it. Her heart broke at that one little word. But a future for her and Logan wasn't possible. She would never take the possibility of a family away from Piper. She loved that little girl.

He dropped her hand like it had been a hot iron. "Congrats," he said as he picked up the piece of paper and began reading the instructions.

Hannah glanced at him. She wanted to say something.

Anything to bring back their happy relationship. But no words came to her. They were already too far down this path. She sighed and grabbed a marker and drew the outline of a stocking on a nearby box.

They worked in silence—each drawing and coloring the boxes. Five minutes later, Logan cleared his throat, breaking the silence.

"So, when's the date?" he asked. They were both crouched down next to each other, decorating their boxes.

Hannah peered over to him. His head was down and he seemed to be coloring a bit too hard. She turned her attention back to her stocking. "I'm not sure. Probably this summer."

"Wow. That's fast."

"Well, we've know each other for three years. So, not really fast for us."

She felt his gaze on her. "Is he what you want?"

Her heart pounded. "What do you mean?"

"I mean, is he what you want or are you doing the classic Hannah?"

Heat raced from her spine and to her cheeks. What did that mean? "What's the classic Hannah?"

Logan laughed. "You can't seriously not know what that means."

Now he was making her mad. "No, as a matter of fact, I don't."

He dropped his marker and studied her. "Running away from problems. That's the classic Hannah."

She gritted her teeth. "I don't run away. How is getting engaged running away? I'm running right to him." The part she'd been coloring was starting to rip through the cardboard so she concentrated her efforts on another part.

"You can't sit there and tell me that you want to marry that guy. You came here to run away from him. If you're engaged now, that tells me one thing. You're running away from something else."

Her gaze whipped to him. "And tell me, oh smart one, what am I running away from now?"

"Do you want me to say it?" His gaze softened as he leaned forward.

Her stomach flipped. Deep down, she knew what he was going to say and she wasn't sure she wanted to hear it. "No," she whispered.

"Why not? Maybe it's time you started facing things even if they're hard."

Hannah couldn't help it; tears formed in her eyes. "I face things."

Logan scoffed. "No, you don't. There are always reasons not to do something. Or a reason to run away."

Hannah whipped around. "What are you talking about? I was there that night at prom. I stayed the hour looking for you. You were the one who ran away."

Logan stood, which put him inches away from her. "Do you honestly think I wanted to leave?" He stared down at her in a way that made her feel raw and exposed. "I had to face the decision I made with Charity, and every decision I've made since then has been for Piper." He reached out and grasped her arm.

The warmth and sensation of him touching her rushed to her heart. It pounded so loud, she could hear it in her ears.

"I never wanted to leave you that night." His voice had grown husky as he leaned down to capture her gaze.

"Logan..."

He dropped his hand and took a step back.

"Please." She gazed up into his eyes, pleading with him to let this go. She didn't know how much longer her willpower would win out against her aching heart. "You said everything you've done since that night has been for Piper. Please, let me go. If you can make it work with Charity, then I can't stand in your way."

His Adam's apple rose and fell as he studied her. "But what if that's not what I want?"

Hannah's cheeks heated. "The truth is, it's what I want. And I'm sure it's what Piper wants." She crouched down and began coloring. From the corner of her eye, she saw Logan's stance tighten then relax.

He joined her on the floor and began coloring again.

She hated the way she had left things. The truth was, she didn't know what the truth was anymore. Her heart felt too disjointed and confused. Everything in her mind told her that Samson was the guy for her. Why couldn't her heart just get up to speed?

LOGAN

It didn't take long for them to finish up with the decorations. Soon, the room was set up and ready for all the kids that were starting to swarm the halls. Thankfully, the tension in the air seemed to dissipate. It seemed that he and Hannah were able to get ahold of their emotions. At least, that is what Logan told himself.

But even with Hannah's relaxed stance and smiles, he still didn't feel good about where he had left things. He should have never come down on her so hard. She didn't deserve it.

"I'm sorry," he said, glancing over to her.

"For what?" She replaced the cap on her marker and turned.

"I should have never said those things to you." He lowered his voice. "It wasn't my place."

The corners of her lips tipped up into a smile. "It's okay. You're right. I do run away when things get tough."

"Yeah, you do."

She reached out and whacked his shoulder. "Hey!"

He grabbed her hand. "I'm kidding."

Her gaze dropped to their clasped hands. "Don't stop doing that," she whispered.

Dropping her hand, he took a step back. He feared what she meant. "Doing what?"

"Telling it to me straight. I need that kick in the pants sometimes." She smiled up at him. "It's nice to know you will always tell me the truth."

He stepped forward. She valued the truth. Maybe it was time he told her. As if sensing his sudden desire to be truthful, she turned her back to him.

"Oh, I forgot," she said as she turned and met his gaze as she held up two sets of clothing. "Apparently, we need to change."

He eyed the linen shirts and khaki pants. "Seriously? They're torn."

"We need to look like the kids who are naughty."

Logan grabbed the clothes that she held out to him. "Who comes up with these things?"

Hannah giggled. "I know, right?"

He smiled at her. This is what he missed. He longed to be in her presence and make her happy—not angry and frustrated. They slipped the costumes on over their clothes. They hung off of Hannah like a potato sack. He dropped his gaze and fought the thoughts that flew into his mind when he pictured her figure. This was *not* what he should be thinking about.

When he turned his attention back to her, she was smiling.

"What?"

She shook her head. "Nothing."

He narrowed his eyes. "What is it?"

She just smiled. "They want us to use the coal to make our faces look dirty." She gripped a piece of charcoal in her hands. "So, maybe I can do yours and you can do mine?"

He studied her. That might not be the best thing to do. "Really?"

She nodded and stepped up to him. Reaching up, she took both of her hands and smacked his cheeks. "There," she giggled.

"Hey!" He glanced over to the window and saw his reflection. Two handprints adorned his cheeks. "I have a feeling that naughty kids don't have handprints on their face. I look like a *World's Best Dad* sweatshirt." He walked closer to her.

"I think you look great," she said, stepping back.

"Oh, no. You're not getting off the hook. Come here."

She laughed and rushed down an aisle, but stopped when she almost collided with Audrey, who raised her eyebrows at the two of them.

"You guys ready?" she asked, eyeing Logan's face.

He steadied his expression. "Yes."

Audrey's silent stare told Logan more than any words could have as she glanced between from him to Hannah. She knew something was going on between them. Just like Logan knew.

"Well, hurry up. Kids are coming."

Logan and Hannah both nodded as she headed toward the door. As soon as she was gone, they both busted up laughing.

Logan waved her over. "Let's get this done."

CHAPTER TWENTY

LOGAN

It was fun manning the game with Hannah. It didn't take long before they fell into a rhythm. Hannah would stand at the line with the kids while Logan retrieved the bean bags that were dusted with coal bits. The kids aimed for the cardboard boxes but instead, the bags flew through the air and thunked against the wall.

Soon the white cinderblock walls looked like a Dalmatian. He was glad he wasn't on the clean-up committee.

"Remind me to high-tail it out of here before Audrey convinces us to stay to clean up," he said as he brought the bean bags back to the waiting hands of the next game goer.

Hannah nodded. "Deal."

He smiled as he returned to his post. Hannah laughed as she leaned in to talk to one of the fifth graders in line. Hannah captured his heart again. The gentle way she spoke to the kids, or the way she engaged them in conversation reminded him of when she'd played with Piper. He knew someday she was going make a great mom.

In no time, their two-hour commitment had ended. Audrey bustled into the room and shooed them out as another couple took their place. Hannah lingered outside the door as Logan pulled off his costume and handed it to a skeptical-looking dad.

"It's fun," Logan said as he turned and headed out the door.

"Well, that was worth it," Hannah said as she fell into step with him. They made their way down the hall and stopped at one of the round hand-washing stations outside the nearest bathroom.

Logan pressed on the activation bar toward the bottom and the water squirted from the nozzles. "It was. I'm happy I did that with you." He smiled over to her as he got his hands wet.

"It reminded me of old times," she said, doing the same.

They washed the coal dust off in silence. Logan cupped his hands and let the water fill up. Splashing it onto his face, he took extra time to rub his cheeks where Hannah had put charcoal. When his face was clean, he grabbed a few paper towels.

Hannah had been much more strategic with washing her face. No doubt, she didn't want to wash off her makeup. A black smear still ran underneath her eye when she moved to release the bar.

"Hang on," Logan said, grabbing a paper towel and wetting it under the water. "You have a little right here." Reaching out, he cupped her chin in his hand. He tried to ignore the surge of feelings that raced through him every time he touched her. After a few dabs of the paper towel, the charcoal streak was removed.

When he brought his gaze up to meet hers, he paused. Her cheeks reddened as she smiled. "Is it gone?"

Emotions boiled up inside of him. Every fiber of his being wanted him to kiss her. To wrap her up in his arms and love her like a man loves a woman. "Hannah, I—"

Her eyes widened as she took a step back, breaking their connection. "No."

His heart broke at that one little word. "But—"

She turned. "I'm going to go find Samson. I suggest you find Charity."

The sound of her shoes clicking on the cement floor marked her retreat. Soon, Logan stood there, all alone. He tilted his face up toward the ceiling and closed his eyes. He needed to stop trying. She'd already told him what she wanted. Why wasn't he listening?

Crumpling the towels up into a ball, he threw them into the nearby trashcan. He knew why. He was never going to stop trying to make it work with Hannah. She was the one. She had always been the one. As much as he wanted to deny it to protect his heart, he couldn't anymore. He loved her. From the deepest depths of his soul—he loved her.

Scoffing, he slapped the drinking fountain button and took a long drink. What good did that do? She had all but told him that she wasn't interested. Not with Charity in the picture.

He squared his shoulders as he headed back down the hall toward the gymnasium. A soft Christmas song could be heard as he neared. He stood in the doorway and glanced around the room. The lights had been dimmed to allow the decorations to shine.

Logan located Piper within a few seconds. Her red curly hair and contagious smile were easy to spot. He leaned against the door frame and thought about Hannah's words. A nagging feeling pulled at the back of his mind. There had to be a way to get the woman he loved and keep his daughter happy. And he wouldn't give up until he found it.

HANNAH

Her stomach was in knots when she walked into the kitchen to find Samson. She rubbed her face in the spot where Logan had touched her earlier. But no matter how hard she tried to wipe away the feeling of his warm fingers against her skin, nothing she did removed that memory. She needed to be careful from now on.

A short woman with dark hair and tanned skin that Hannah could only dream of tsk-tsked her as she hurried past. "Hair net, my dear. We don't need any of those children eating one of those golden strands of yours."

Hannah's hand flew up to her head as she glanced around sheepishly. "Sorry. I'm looking for Samson. Have you seen him?"

The woman waved at her to follow. "No time to stop, honey. I must walk and talk, or I will have a riot on my hands. The refreshment table doesn't fill itself."

Feeling the urgency the woman was projecting, Hannah quickened her pace to fall into step with her. After the woman barked a few orders at a mom with the green sparkly sweater, she glanced back at Hannah. "Who did you say you were looking for?"

"Samson."

The woman raised her finely plucked eyebrows. "I haven't seen him. After I corrected him while he was massacring the watermelon I gave him to cut up, he high-tailed it out of here." She sighed as she glanced at up at Hannah. "How hard is it to cut one-inch circles?"

Hannah just nodded as if she understood, but she really didn't. "Do you know which direction he went?"

The woman waved her hand toward the back door.

"Thank you," Hannah called over her shoulder and headed

in the direction the woman had motioned. Pressing the silver handle, Hannah stepped outside. The setting sun washed the sky in yellows and oranges. "Samson?" she called out as the door clicked closed behind her.

"Samson?" she called again.

"Over here," Samson said as he rounded the corner of the building.

Hannah smiled. "Why are you out here?"

He folded his arms across his chest. "Blanca is crazy. Once she came over to inspect my work, she started yelling at me in Spanish and took my knife away."

"Yeah, I can see that. She's pretty intense."

Samson nodded as he reached out and wrapped his arm around Hannah. "And those kids are crazy. I mean, one kid almost punched me in the stomach when the mini doughnut bowl got too low." He leaned back and widened his eyes.

Hannah laughed. "Yeah, kids can get crazy sometimes. Especially when sugar's involved."

He pulled her against his chest again. "Makes me miss Ohio and our quiet life. When are we going back? My mother is hosting this amazing dinner party in New York. I was thinking we could fly there first and then make it back to Ohio for the Christmas party the company is throwing."

Hannah wiggled until he released his grip. "Samson, I'm here to visit my family. I'm spending this time with my mom, and then Christmas day I'm going to my dad's."

He studied her. "But why? It's okay. You've done your daughterly duty. You're always saying how much you dislike spending time with your mom, anyway."

Hannah took a step back. "I don't always say that."

Samson gave her a pointed look. "Yes, you do."

"Well, that might have been true, but things have changed. We're trying to mend our relationship."

Samson sighed. In the same way he did when his driver told him there was traffic. It was a *this is going to inconvenience me* sigh. Hannah wasn't sure what she thought about being on the receiving end of it. She studied him. What she did know was, she didn't like the idea that he wasn't open to spending time with her family.

"What was that earlier?" she asked.

His phone chimed so he pulled it out. After a few seconds, he spoke up. "What was what?" His gaze stayed fixed on the screen.

Hannah fought the urge to take it and chuck it in the dumpster. "When you said you didn't like being around kids. Did you mean it?"

Whatever was on his phone had his undivided attention. "Yeah. Kids are loud and sticky. And they cost a lot of money."

A tingle raced down Hannah's spine. "But our kids won't be like that."

He snorted. "Our kids?"

Stepping away from him, Hannah wrapped her arms around her chest. This conversation was not going well. "Yes. Our kids."

Samson was silent. When she glanced back, he'd turned his attention to her. "You want to have kids?"

Was he serious? "You don't?"

"Eh," he said as he shrugged and turned his attention back to the phone. "I'd be fine if we didn't have them."

Hannah's gaze focused on the parking lot where a mom and a dad and two daughters were walking arm in arm to their silver minivan. It was everything she'd ever wanted in a family since she was a kid. Her heart sank. And the man standing behind her, the one she was engaged to, didn't want this.

At that moment, she didn't want to think about it anymore. No conclusion she could draw from this would be good.

Perhaps, for the time being, it was best to push this far from her mind. No matter how much Logan's voice echoed in her mind. She wasn't running away—she was being wise.

Two arms wrapped around her waist and pulled her close. She tried to relax as Samson nuzzled her neck. "Why are you so far away?" he breathed into her ear.

His closeness no longer sent tingles up her spine as it had done in the past. She sighed. She really was bothered by the fact he didn't want kids. Shaking her head, she pushed the feelings of doubt away. It was Christmastime—a time of cheer. She was sure Samson would change his mind when the time came.

She turned and allowed him to press his lips to hers. When she pulled away, she glanced up. "You'll change your mind about babies when you see ours," she said, glancing up at him.

He pinched his lips together. "We still on that? Come on, Han. You can't say you'd rather be home changing diapers and wiping noses over flying to Paris on a whim? With babies, we'd be tied down." His phone chimed, so he kept one arm around her and glanced at the screen in his other hand.

"Samson, who's talking to you?"

He locked his phone and shoved it into his pocket. "Just Mom. She's wondering if we will make it to her holiday party. She wants to show off her future daughter-in-law."

Hannah studied him. "You told her we won't be able to make it, right?"

The smile on his face seemed a bit too forced. "Of course. It's important for us to be here." He wrapped his free arm back around her and pulled her close. "Now, where were we?"

Hannah allowed him to embrace her. As she stood there, she forced her mind to relax. Maybe she was being a bit ridiculous. After all, he told his mom that her family was a priority right now. That did make her feel important.

And so what if he didn't want to have kids right now? Look at how quickly he changed his mind about the holidays? As she wrapped her arms around him, she breathed in his cologne. But as much as she tried to force the feeling of home in his embrace, it just wasn't there.

CHAPTER TWENTY-ONE

HANNAH

People began to trickle out of the building as Hannah and Samson stood there. She tried to keep her gaze off of the hyped-up kids and stressed-out parents. It didn't matter how hard parenting looked, she knew it was what she wanted. She turned to smile at all the rosy-cheeked, sticky-faced kids.

Her heart raced when Logan and Piper came through the door. He had her on his shoulders as she held a giant, rainbow-colored teddy bear. Charity followed right behind them, grounding Hannah back to reality. She squared her shoulders as they approached.

"Miss Hannah! Miss Hannah! Look what I won," Piper said, wiggling around as she tried to get off Logan's shoulders.

"Pip, hang on." Logan laughed as he bent over and helped her down.

Piper raced up to Hannah with the bear extended. "Isn't it amazing?" She leaned down and kissed it on the cheeks.

Hannah crouched down and looked it over. "I don't

know..." She glanced up at Piper, whose face fell. Then Hannah smiled. "I don't think it's amazing. I think it's fantabulistic." She patted the teddy on its head, and Piper glowed.

"I can't believe I won it. I didn't think I was going to, but I didn't give up at the ring toss, and I won." Her smile looked as if it was going to explode off her face.

"Okay. Okay, Piper. Calm down. It's just a bear," Charity piped up from behind. Hannah fought the urge to glare at her. It wasn't like she'd notice, though. She was too busy glancing around sheepishly at all the parents who were walking by and staring at them.

"Well, I think it's great. We should celebrate." Hannah smiled.

"Actually, Han. Don't you remember? Bachelor and bachelorette parties?" Logan glanced down at her and tapped his watch.

Hannah's stomach sank. She'd forgotten. "Right." Peering into Piper's disappointed face, she smiled. "Rain check?"

Piper studied her. "Only if we can play with Truly and Samantha. I want them to meet Rainy." She reached out and patted the bear's head.

Hannah stuck out her pinky. "I promise."

Piper gripped her finger with her own and brought it up and down a few times. "Deal."

Standing, Hannah glanced up at Logan. "What time is it, anyway?"

He twisted his wrist. "Seven thirty."

"Crap. I need to be at the first bar by eight." She glanced behind her to Samson, who was back on his phone. "Can you make it home by yourself?"

"Actually," Charity said, stepping forward, "I was hoping to tag along with you."

Hannah glanced at her, then over to Piper. "Really? I figured you'd want to spend some time with your daughter."

If Charity noticed Hannah's tone, she didn't show it. "I've spent all day with her. I'm ready for some girl time. And besides, I haven't seen Sandy since high school." She widened her eyes as if she were trying to convince Hannah.

Hannah took a step back. Didn't she know that wouldn't work on her? "Um..." When she glanced over to Logan, she studied his expression.

"How about Charity goes with you, and I'll take Samson with me?" he offered.

"I want to go," Piper said, glancing around.

"Sorry, sweetie. Adults only," Charity said.

Hannah tried not to let her heart break from the sad look that swept over Piper's face. "Tomorrow, we can play with my dolls. Okay?" she whispered to Piper, who nodded and went back to hugging her bear.

"What do you think?" Hannah asked as she glanced back to Samson.

"Beats hanging out with your mom all night, sure."

Hannah tried not to let it bother her that he'd say that. Instead, she turned around. "Sounds good. Okay, you're coming with me." She nodded to Charity.

"And I've just gotta drop off Piper with my mom, and then we'll head out."

Hannah tried to ignore the skeptical look on Samson's face as she waved at Charity to follow her. Pulling out her phone, she hit Bert's number.

"Ready?" he asked after one ring.

"Yep."

"Be there in five."

"Perfect."

She hung up the phone and slipped it into her purse. She tried to ignore the raised eyebrows of Charity.

"Who was that?"

Hannah brushed her hand against the nearby bench and sat down. "Bert. He's a cab driver." She pulled her purse up into her lap.

Charity did the same. "Ah. No car?"

Hannah shook her head. "Didn't rent one this time."

Silence filled the air. Hannah willed Bert to hurry.

"So, why did you come back?" Charity asked.

Hannah turned to look at her. Was she serious? "My mom lives here."

"Last time I heard, you and your mom were no longer speaking."

Heat raced to Hannah's cheeks. How much did this woman know about her personal life? "Well, we've had our problems. But we are trying to work on it."

"Convenient," Charity whispered, as she glanced out to the parking lot.

"Excuse me?" Hannah leaned forward.

Charity turned and smiled at her. "Nothing."

Anger filled Hannah's stomach. "No. Not nothing. Why is it convenient that I came back for the *holidays* to visit my mom?"

Charity's smile grew wider. "Nothing. It's fine. Geez."

Hannah wanted to punch the girl. Here, she had an amazing husband and daughter, and yet she chose to leave them, all for selfish reasons. And she had the gall to call her shady.

Before Hannah could push the conversation forward, Bert pulled up next to the curb. He rolled the window down. "Ready, girlie?"

If he only knew. Hannah stood and made her way to the

cab with Charity right behind her. She motioned to the back and pulled open the passenger door. Bert looked at her with wide eyes as she buckled.

Hannah returned his look. She hoped he'd sense her need to get away from Charity. He paused and then nodded.

"All right, Hannah and Hannah's friend. Where are we off to?"

"To the Admiral Arms," Hannah said.

Bert nodded. "On it."

LOGAN

Logan stood in the doorway of the Captain's Cabin, staring at the massive party that Veronica had put together. He knew he should have called and canceled her services when she laughed after he told her money was no issue. He gulped as a waitress in a tight sequined dress walked past, holding a tray of what could only be astronomically expensive cigars.

A squeal sounded behind him. He turned to see Veronica's beaming face as she rushed over to him. "I love you," she proclaimed as she grabbed his arm and shook it.

"Veronica... this is not what we talked about." He nodded around the room.

She stuck out her bottom lip. "It's not that bad. Come on. Never has a client told me there was no price limit to a party." She pulled on his arm so he followed her.

"I rented out the entire restaurant just for the party. I had all the food flown in from New York's finest restaurants—"

"Veron—"

"Oh, come on, Logan. You're rich now. Embrace it."

He shushed her as he glanced around. This was not what he wanted.

Veronica rolled her eyes. "Relax. Everyone knows. Mrs.

Trumble got ahold of the news; now all of North Carolina knows."

Logan's stomach sank. "What?"

"The real question is, why did you want to keep it a secret?" she asked as a man in a tuxedo approached her with a tray of tiny hors d'oeuvres. She stuck one in her mouth and groaned. "Oh, my— you have to try this," she said, shoving one toward Logan's lips.

Before he could step back, she pushed it into his mouth. For a moment, he considered spitting it out, but when the buttery texture hit his tongue, he was entranced. It was the best—whatever it was—he'd ever tasted.

"Veronica. That was amazing."

Veronica's eyes sparkled. "I know, right? This is your future life." She smiled as she waved her hand toward the elegant wallpaper and tableclothed tables.

A feeling settled in his gut. The problem was, this wasn't what he wanted.

"Dude." Jimmy's voice filtered through the slow jazz that carried around the room.

Turning, Logan saw the opened lips and bugged eyes of his best friend. "You like it?" he asked.

Jimmy glanced over to him. "I'm gonna have to get married more often if this is the kind of party you throw me."

Logan punched his arm. "I only do this once," he said. He did have to admit, he liked how much his friend seemed to appreciate what he'd done. Or at least, what Veronica had done with his money.

"This is insane," Jimmy said as he limped over and took some food off of the tray that a waiter was carrying. After a few chews, his eyes closed. "Dude. This tastes like heaven." He opened his eyes. "I can't believe that you can afford this now."

"Afford what?" Samson asked, walking up next to them.

Jimmy's gaze swept over him. "Who are you?"

"Jimmy, this is Hannah's fiancé, Samson. Samson, this is the guy that's getting hitched tomorrow."

The two men shook hands.

"Nice party," Samson said, glancing around.

Jimmy clapped Logan on the back. "Thanks to my loaded buddy, we can really party in style now."

Samson eyed him. "Loaded?"

Jimmy nodded and leaned toward Samson. "We're talking north of millions."

"Jimmy," Logan said, glaring at him. This was getting awful. Was this his fate now? Walking around town and having people stare at him, seeing only dollar amounts?

Samson eyed him. "Family money?"

Logan just nodded. He didn't want to talk about it and he *really* didn't want to talk about it with Hannah's fiancé.

Veronica clapped her hands, and Logan was thankful for the interruption. Turning away from Samson, he studied her as she stood in the middle of the room, surrounded by all of Jimmy's friends.

"Welcome to the bachelor party for Jimmy. We have a fun night planned. So, find a seat so the food can be served." She smiled as she glanced around the room. "Everything has been paid for. There's a free bar." She motioned to the bartender standing behind the counter, flipping bottles in the air.

Half the party goers hooted and hollered.

"After dinner, we have a high stakes poker game set up." She waved to the green velvet-covered tables in the back room. "And for those who don't wish to participate, we have the lounge area where there are games and TV." She nodded toward the glass-enclosed lounge area.

"Cigars are free, so help yourself." She smiled as she stepped away from the group.

"Well, let's grab a table," Jimmy said, limping over to the round table at the front of the room. He pulled out the chair that had a huge balloon tied to it. The word *Congrats* was scrawled across it. It shifted in the vent air above.

Logan went to follow him, hoping Samson would find a different table. But, when he pulled out his chair and Samson did the same, Logan tried to stifle a groan.

Once they were seated, men in tuxedos emerged and delivered dinner to all the guests. When they uncovered their plates, Jimmy let out a whoop. "Steak and potatoes. Ah, man, you shouldn't have."

Logan just smiled and dug in. But by the time his plate was cleaned, he was cheering inside. It was the best food he'd had in a while.

As they leaned back to stretch out their stomachs, the waiters returned and the dirty plates were whisked way. After the chocolate cake was delivered and devoured, they started to leave their seats to wander around the enormous restaurant.

It was strange to be here all alone. All the empty tables with no customers to fill them. As Logan eyed the far poker tables, he debated about grabbing a seat. A few guys had already settled in, and the dealer had started shuffling the cards.

"Come on, man," Jimmy said, clapping his hand on Logan's shoulder. "I wanna see if I can win some of that money of yours." He shot him a smile.

"Will you stop doing that?" Logan asked, following behind Jimmy.

"Doing what?"

"Telling people I'm loaded. I don't like it." He pulled out the chair next to the one Jimmy was getting ready to sit down on.

"Why? You should be proud to have it."

Logan's stomach lurched. That wasn't true. "It's not mine.

It was my dad's, and he worked hard to earn it." He swallowed as a lump grew in his throat. "I haven't done anything to earn it." Truth was, the money was just a reminder that the relationship he had wished for all those Christmases ago was no longer a reality.

He turned to see Jimmy staring at him.

"Your old man gave you this money. He trusted you. Plus, he was probably trying to make up for all those years he wasn't in your life." Jimmy nodded toward the dealer who had handed him some cards. "It's time you started doing stuff for yourself and Piper. After all the things you've gone through these last few years, you deserve to treat yourself."

Logan grabbed the cards that the dealer put in front of him. Jimmy's words echoed in his mind. He knew that he was right. It was pretty much what his dad had said weeks before his death as they sat across from the lawyer. Problem was, he knew it was the right thing to do in his mind, but his heart just wasn't having it.

"Mind if I join you?" Samson asked from beside Logan.

Turning, Logan nodded. "Be my guest."

Samson pulled out the chair. "Thanks."

Grateful for something other than his dad's money to talk about, Logan diverted all of his energy to the guy sitting next to him. He'd just ignore the fact that this guy was the fiancé to the girl he loved.

CHAPTER TWENTY-TWO

HANNAH

Bert pulled up in front of the Admiral Arms. Hannah sighed. She was ready to get this evening over with. Turning to Charity, she smiled. "Ready?"

Charity nodded, opened the door, and stepped out onto the sidewalk. When she shut the door, Hannah turned back to Bert, who was eyeing her.

"Who's your new friend?" He tipped his head toward Charity.

Hannah dug around in her purse for some money. All she had was a twenty. "Here. Can you stick around? I have a feeling a lot of these ladies are going to get hammered."

Bert nodded as he slipped the twenty into his front pocket. "Are you one of those ladies?"

Hannah shook her head. She hated drinking. Well, she hated the feeling that drinking caused the next day. "Nope. Someone has to be the sober one."

Bert nodded. "You didn't tell me who that was."

Hannah's stomach flipped. "She's Logan's ex-wife."

Bert leaned down as if to get a good look at her. "Logan? The boy next door?"

"Yes."

"She's back?"

Hannah nodded and fought the urge to say that was pretty obvious.

Bert settled back on the chair. "Eh. Won't last. I wouldn't put my money on that relationship."

Hannah stared at him. "You've seen this before?"

"Honey, in my experience, issues don't just disappear with time. If they had problems before—they'll still have them. Beside, women like her"—he nodded toward Charity who was pulling out a tube of lipstick from her purse—"don't change."

Hannah swallowed. As much as she wanted to believe Bert, she wasn't sure if she could let her heart hope. Besides, Piper was involved, and she wouldn't do anything to hurt that little girl. She pulled on the handle and allowed the cool, salty air to waft into the car. "Let's hope you're right," she said.

The music blared from the speakers as they pulled open the door to the bar and walked in. It was a twangy pop song. The air smelled like alcohol and desperation. It almost made Hannah shiver.

"I'm going to go powder my nose," Charity said as she veered off to the bathroom.

"Okay," Hannah said as she glanced around.

"Hannah Banana!" Sandy screamed as she danced up to Hannah. She was already a bit tipsy.

"I see you've started without me," she said, returning the hug that Sandy had flung on her.

"You made it."

"Yes. Is everyone here?"

Sandy pulled off of Hannah and glanced around. "I think

so." She sauntered over to the bar and grabbed a bag. "Tricia wanted me to give this to you. It's the garb for the party."

Hannah eyed Sandy. This wasn't good. When she opened the bag, and took in all of the male-shaped goodies, she clamped it shut and set it down next to her. "Maybe later," she said.

Sandy just laughed. "The night is young. I'll have you eating those gummies in no time."

Hannah just smiled. "You can try." But from the way Sandy was swaying side to side, someone needed to be responsible tonight.

"Hannah," a tight voice said from behind her.

She turned. Her mom's lips were drawn taught as she stood there in a white blouse tucked into a dark blue pencil skirt.

"Hey, Mom. You look great." Definitely a difference from her mom's standard dark blue scrubs.

Her mom gave her a small smile. "Thanks. Drew picked it out." Her mom's shoulders loosened. "I wasn't going to come, but he convinced me it would be good to get out."

Hannah eyed her mom. She needed to meet this Drew character. He was getting her mom to do more things in the last few days than Hannah had ever been able to get her mom to do in her whole life. Wrapping her arm around her mom's shoulders, Hannah pulled her into a hug.

"I'm just glad you came, Mom."

Her mom tensed, then relaxed. "Me too, sweetie."

"Miss Bell," Sandy screamed as she rushed over and enveloped her mom in a hug. "I'm so glad you came to party with us."

"Well, that was disgusting," Charity said as she walked up to them.

Sandy pulled back. "Charity Monson? What are you doing here?"

Charity quirked an eyebrow. "I'm here to spend time with Logan and Piper. Hannah invited me along while Logan took her fiancé to Jimmy's party."

Sandy's gaze fell to Hannah. "Wow. Hannah didn't say anything about that."

Charity winced as a particularly tipsy guy walked past her, bumping his shoulder into hers. "Well, it was decided only about an hour ago." Then she paused. "It's okay that I'm here. Right?"

Sandy glanced back to her. "Sure. I guess." She gave Charity a small smile, but the disdain in Sandy's voice could be heard above the chatter of all the customers at the bar.

Charity gave a sweet smile. "Wonderful. I'm going to get a drink." She turned and headed toward the counter.

"You invited her?" Sandy asked, whipping around.

"Yeah. Why?" Sandy was acting strange. Why was this a bad thing?

"Didn't Logan tell you?" Sandy asked. Hannah's mom was shaking her head.

"No. What?"

"Oh, honey. It was bad. Charity apparently cheated on him with one of his coworkers and then she emptied their bank account and took off. It took him a year to track her down so he could get her to sign the divorce papers. By then, she'd already spent everything she'd taken and would only sign the papers if he paid her more," Sandy said.

Hannah's stomach churned. "What about Piper?" That poor little girl. How could a mom do something like that?

Hannah's mom shook her head. "She didn't care about Piper. Never asked for custody. Gave it all to Logan. Ginger said she's always promising to come get Piper, but then never showing up."

Hannah eyed Charity, who was flirting with the bartender

behind the counter. He nodded his head as she reached across and grazed his arm. Frustration and anger boiled up. Who would do that to Logan? He was the best guy she'd ever known. The fact that he faced his responsibility was one quality she loved about him.

Charity wasn't going to find a better guy anywhere. And he was a great dad. Hannah fisted her hands. There was a feeling in her stomach that was growing stronger with every thought of Logan. It was one she could no longer ignore. Charity needed to go.

Then she inwardly groaned. But she'd all but pushed them together. Why had she been so insistent that they make things work? If she'd only known what Charity had done, Hannah would have been more reserved. Now, Logan and Charity were together. Because of her. Maybe she did need that drink after all.

Sandy pulled away once she saw some more guests arrive. She promised to be right back. Standing next to her mom, Hannah wrapped her arms around her stomach.

"What's wrong?" her mom asked, peering down at her.

Hannah shook her head. She wasn't sure she was ready to talk about her giant mistake right now. "Nothing. Just thirsty, I think."

Her mom nodded and headed over to the bar. "I'll grab you a Coke."

"Thanks," Hannah said as she took a few steps over to the wall and leaned against it. Why did she feel so sick? It had to be because of what Charity might do to Piper. What else could it be?

LOGAN

Logan held up his cards and looked at them. Three queens

and two kings. He was trying to hide the excitement that was coursing through his veins. This was his first good hand. He didn't want to give it away.

"I see your bet, and I raise you fifty," Jimmy said, throwing a few poker chips onto the already heaping pile. It was down to Jimmy, Samson, and Logan.

Logan glanced back down to his cards—just to make sure they hadn't changed—then fiddled with his chips. "I'll see your bet and raise it another hundred."

All eyes turned to Samson. He glanced at his cards, then over to the pile on the table. "I see your bets and call."

"Excellent," the dealer said. "Let's see the cards."

Logan laid his hand down on the table. Samson and Jimmy did the same. Whooping, Logan pumped his fist into the air. He'd won.

Jimmy groaned. "Ah, man," he said as he folded his arms. "It's my party. You couldn't just let me win?"

Logan smiled as he pulled the pile of chips toward him. "Here, go buy something pretty," he said, pulling one from the pile and setting it in front of Jimmy.

A phone chimed next to him. Glancing over, Logan's stomach sank as Samson pulled his phone out of his pocket. Was it Hannah calling? His mouth went dry as he adjusted his chips. He needed to stop thinking about Hannah right now. She'd moved on. He needed to remember that.

"Party going well?" he asked, hoping he sounded normal.

Samson looked up from the screen. "Huh?"

"Sandy's party. Is it going well?" He nodded toward Samson's phone.

"How would I know that?"

Logan nodded to the dealer who'd set a stack of cards in front of him. "You mean, that's not Hannah?"

Samson shook his head. "No. It's not Hannah. It's my travel agent."

For the first time in a long time, Logan felt optimistic. Did he dare hope that Samson was leaving? "You're going somewhere?"

Samson nodded. "Yes. As soon as I can, I'm whisking Hannah away to New York."

Logan paused. Hannah was leaving? "The day before Christmas Eve? She's not going to the wedding?"

Samson turned his attention back to his phone and his fingers flew against the screen as he typed. Then he turned off his phone and stuck it back into his pocket. "She'll be okay. Once I get her there, she'll come around. Besides, this is the socialite party of the year. It's really important to my family."

Logan shuffled his cards around in his hand. "But she wants to be here with her family."

From the corner of his eye, he saw Samson tense. "Hannah doesn't know what she wants. Once we're married, she'll start seeing things my way."

Logan took the seven and five from his hand, laid it down in front of him, and nodded toward the dealer. When two new cards were deposited in front of him, he picked them up and almost sighed. The two and jack were not what he needed.

"What sort of things is she not seeing your way?" He tried to keep his voice calm even though he desperately wanted to know.

Samson picked up his new cards and shuffled them around. "Kids. She wants kids."

Logan threw a poker chip into the pile. "You don't?"

"No. Kids are messy and complicate life," Samson said, shaking his head like even thinking about kids was disgusting. "But yet again, I'll get her to see my way once we're married."

Logan eyed him. "You seem to think that marriage is the solution to issues."

Samson laughed. "It's not what works for everyone, but it will work for us."

Logan tapped his cards against the table and glanced around. Since when was Hannah such a pushover? Did she act different around Samson? She'd always struck him as a strong, independent person. Why would she change now?

"Fold," he said when the bet got to him. He no longer felt like playing. His stomach was in knots when he thought about Samson and Hannah and the waiting travel agent. It ate at his heart. He didn't want her to go, but what else could he do? She didn't want him, that was clear.

As he watched Samson raise the bet, he clenched his jaw. She wanted the guy sitting next to him. The one who wanted to manipulate her into doing what he wanted. Logan folded his arms. He needed say some things to Hannah before she left. As he glanced up to the clock, he wished time would speed up before he lost his nerve.

CHAPTER TWENTY-THREE

HANNAH

Sandy had convinced the DJ to play all the nineties songs they'd grown up loving. Soon, a group of women raced up to the microphone and began screaming into it. Hannah sighed and settled down on a barstool that was a few spots down from Charity who, after a few drinks, became very chatty.

Poor Melissa, Sandy's younger sister, was on the receiving end of that chattiness. She forced a smile at Charity, who was leaning in.

"You remind me of my roommate," Charity slurred as she pointed her finger at Melissa.

"Oh, that's nice."

Charity slapped her hand down on the counter. "No, it's not. She was awful." Charity reached out and touched Melissa's hair. "Your hair even looks like hers."

Melissa moved to inch away, but Charity dropped her hand and leaned back.

"Don't matter anymore. I'm with Logan now." She reached

out and grabbed her shot glass in front of her. "Logan," she mumbled.

Melissa glanced over to Hannah, who just shrugged. This woman really couldn't hold her liquor.

Just when Melissa moved to stand, Charity shot her hand out and patted Melissa's arm. "He's loaded now, you know that?"

Hannah's ears pricked at the mention of Logan's money.

"That's nice," Melissa said.

"Like, lots of millions, loaded." Charity hiccuped and smiled. "I'm gonna be a rich woman."

Hannah's stomach soured. What did that mean? She slid over the remaining seats. "You're going to be rich?" she asked as she leaned toward Charity.

Her empty gaze fell on Hannah. "Yes. Why do you think I came back? He thinks I just found out, but"—she hiccuped again—"I knew all along."

Heat raced from her spine as she studied the awful woman in front of her. "Not to be with Piper?"

Charity scoffed. "As soon as we're married again, she's going to a prep school." Charity giggled and pushed her fingers against her lips. "Whoops. Don't tell Logan."

Hannah stared at her. What an awful person. Her mother was never perfect, but at least she wanted Hannah around. Piper deserved someone better than this.

But before she could think about what she was going to do with this information, Sandy started shouting her name into the microphone. For some reason, the tipsy Sandy thought it was a good idea that they sing *Big Girls Don't Cry* karaoke style—even though the DJ repeatedly said this wasn't a karaoke bar.

Hannah obliged. After all, this was Sandy's bachelorette party. When the song was finished, she checked the schedule and informed all the party goers it was time to head to the next bar.

After shoving all the women into the cabs that were lined up against the street, Hannah pulled open the passenger door to Bert's cab and jumped in. They made it to the next bar in record time. The rest of the night was filled with drinking, singing, some attempts at mini golf, and puking. As Hannah watched it all unfold in front of her, she was glad she'd chosen to sit this one out.

By midnight, she crawled into Bert's cab between Charity and her mom. Charity moaned when she slammed the door. Silence filled the air as Bert pulled away from the curb. As Hannah watched the lights fly by, her thoughts turned to Charity and her confession.

What was she going to do? Logan had to know his ex's intentions. Hannah clenched her jaw. And she'd pushed so hard for them to get back together.

"What's wrong, Hannah?" Her mom's soft voice broke through the silence.

Turning, Hannah glanced over to her mom. She looked tired. "Nothing."

Her mom quirked an eyebrow. "Hannah, what's wrong?"

Glancing up, she saw Bert studying her through the rearview mirror. He gave her a small smile of encouragement.

"I'm worried about a decision I made," Hannah said, turning back to her mom.

"To marry Samson?"

Hannah shook her head. "Involving Logan."

Her mom grew quiet, so Hannah looked over to her. "You care about him, don't you?"

Charity was snoring by now, her head propped up on the window and a trail of drool making its way down her chin. She was passed out so wouldn't hear Hannah's confession. Tears stung her eyes as she looked out the window again.

"I do, Mom. So much."

Her mom's hand engulfed hers. "I always had the suspicion. Only true love has the capability to break your heart like this."

Hannah wiped a tear as she turned to look at her mom. "True love?"

Her mom nodded.

"Mom, I don't love Logan."

"Hannah." Her mom reached out and wiped another tear. "I think you do."

Hannah broke her gaze and turned her attention back outside as the words settled in her mind. Love. Did she love Logan? Butterflies erupted in her stomach at the thought. A smile played on her lips. She did. She loved Logan so much that it hurt to breathe.

Turning back around, she smiled at her mom. "You're right. I do."

Her mom pushed a strand of hair from her face. "So the question is, what are you going to do now that you know?"

Hannah straightened in her seat. "I'm going to tell him."

Her mom clapped her hands. "Perfect!"

Bert pulled into Hannah's driveway. Her mom pulled on the handle. "I'm going to bed. Busy day tomorrow. I think there are a few things you need to take care of." She nodded toward the Blakes' residence.

Hannah's eyes widened. "What? Now?"

Her mom smiled. "No time like the present," she said as she stepped out, leaving the door open as she made her way to the walkway and disappeared into the house.

The smile on Hannah's lips grew bigger the more she thought about Logan and confessing to him that she loved him.

It had always been him. She wanted to be a part of his life now and forever. She wanted to be there for Piper. She wanted to be a family. As she moved to slide out of the cab, a hand shot out and grabbed Hannah's arm.

Startled, she glanced back to see Charity staring at her. Hannah's stomach sank. Did she hear? "How are you feeling?" she asked, giving her a small smile.

Charity's gaze turned icy. "I heard," she said with her voice low and threatening.

Hannah steeled her nerves. "Heard what?"

"Your declaration of love for Logan."

Hannah glanced over to Bert, who was watching their interaction. She swallowed. "Well, it's true, and I'm not going to deny it."

Charity laughed. "If you tell Logan, trust me, things won't go over well." She tightened her grasp, digging her fingernails into Hannah's arm.

"Excuse me?"

"If you tell Logan..." She narrowed her eyes, and her gaze filled with anger.

"Are you threatening me?"

Charity's laugh sent a chill through Hannah. "Threatening? No. Promising. See, I'm Piper's mom. Not you. I have the ability to make their life a living hell. If Logan dumps me for you, I will take him back to court."

Hannah felt sick. This wasn't what she wanted. "But, Logan has full custody."

Charity straightened and glanced out the window. "For now. And even if I can't win, I will never stop fighting."

Hannah tried to swallow, but her mouth was dry. "Charity, don't do that. Not to Piper."

Her gaze fell back to Hannah. "Then leave us alone. Go off and marry Samson. Forget about Logan."

Hannah fought back the tears that were filling her eyes. Realization settled in her stomach. If she loved Logan and Piper like she did, then there was only one thing she could do. She needed to walk away. "Fine. I will go. But, please, don't send Piper to a prep school. She loves you. All she wanted was to play American Girl dolls with you."

Charity snorted. "Those stupid dolls? I'm not wasting my money on them."

Hannah glanced over to her.

Charity sighed and raised her hands "Okay, I'll think about not sending her to a prep school. As long as you leave us alone."

Hannah nodded and slid out the open door, her heart breaking with every movement. Charity staggered out of the car as well and made her way across the Blakes' yard and disappeared inside.

Hannah stood there, not sure what to do. She feared what would happen to her heart if she walked into her house and shut the door.

"Hannah," Bert called from the passenger window.

She bent down and glanced inside.

"Why are you doing this?"

A tear fell. "I have to, Bert."

He shook his head. "No, you don't. Don't let that awful woman win."

Frustration from the night boiled over. "What do you know? You're a cab driver. Just leave me and my problems alone." She stepped back, stifling a sob.

"Hann—"

"Go," she said as she turned.

There were a few seconds of silence. Hannah's heart pounded in her chest. She didn't have to look to know that Bert had pulled out of the driveway. Soon, she was alone. All alone.

LOGAN

Logan sat at the kitchen table, nursing his headache. He wished he could blame it on the liquor and cigars, but he'd only had a few drinks—nothing to cause him this pain. It must be from sitting next to Samson all night. Rubbing his temples, he glanced over at the clock. Twelve thirty. Where were the ladies?

The front door slammed, causing Logan to jump from his seat. As he rounded the corner, he saw Charity slip into the basement. His heart sped up. If she was home, that meant one thing—Hannah was home.

Peering out the front window, he saw the cab pull out of her driveway and speed down the street, leaving Hannah standing in the yard. She was staring up at the sky. This was his chance.

He opened the front door and steeled his nerves. He couldn't wait to tell her Samson's intentions. It felt like an eternity as he crossed his yard and was standing next to her. She had her arms wrapped around her chest and her face tilted upwards. It was as if she was in a trance.

"Hey," he said, reaching out and touching her shoulder. Tingles raced up his arm from touching her.

She jumped and turned. Her eyes were puffy—as if she'd been crying. "Logan?" Her voice was rough.

"What's wrong?" He stepped toward her. The urge to protect her surged through his body. All he wanted to do was wrap her up in his arms.

But before he could get close, she moved away. "Don't..." She glanced up at him.

He didn't like the look she was giving him. It was the same one he'd seen a few days ago when she was sitting next to his mom. "Hannah, what happened?" What brought on this sudden chilly disposition?

Hannah glanced over at his house. "Where's Charity?"

Logan shrugged. "In bed, I'm guessing." Then he studied her. "Did she say something?"

Hannah's face flushed, but she shook her head. "No, nothing."

Dipping down to catch her gaze, Logan reached out. "Hannah, you have to believe me when I say that I don't have feelings for Charity anymore. That ship has sailed."

Hannah shoulders tightened. This wasn't going how he wanted. Words got jumbled in his mind. He needed to bring her back. He knew she had feelings for him. Why wouldn't she just admit it?

"Samson's taking you back to his house tomorrow. He doesn't care that you want to spend time with your mom and dad. Plus, he doesn't want to have kids," came tumbling out. He pinched his lips as he studied her. Inside, he was trying to fight the feeling that he'd just tattled on Samson, but he was desperate.

Her eyes widened as she stared at him. "You talked about me with Samson?"

Ugh. The tone of her voice and the look in her eyes told him that he'd made a mistake. "He told me. Bragged is probably the better way to put it."

Hannah turned away. The moonlight lit up her profile as she stared at the ground.

"He's not good for you." Logan reached out again. Why wouldn't she just admit it?

"He's not good for me? What do you know?" She whipped around and glared at him.

Logan studied her gaze. Behind the anger was sadness.

Why was she sad? "You can't be serious. You have to know." He wasn't going to hide that he loved her anymore.

Hannah shook her head. "All I know is, I love Samson and he loves me. We're getting married and that's it. We'll discuss having kids when the time's right. Besides, I think it's best that I leave tomorrow after the wedding." She took another step back.

"What? What about Christmas Eve? What about your mom?" His voice dropped as emotions clung to his throat. "What about me?"

"It's what's best for you and me. And Piper."

He glanced up at her. He heard her voice falter at the mention of his daughter. Something had happened. Why wouldn't she just tell him? Before he could ask, she turned and started walking toward the house.

"Hannah." He rushed over to her. He couldn't let things end like this. She was supposed to be with him. "Hannah." He reached out and grabbed her elbow.

"Leave me alone. We're done. We should have taken our cue from the cosmos. We are not supposed to be together." She gave him a weak smile. "Just leave it at that."

"But...I can't." How was he going to make her see?

"I'll see you at the wedding." She turned and walked up the front stoop.

"Hannah—"

"Good night." Her voice was weak. She pulled open the door and slipped inside.

Logan stood there, paralyzed. He wanted to confess to her that he loved her. He wanted to tell her she was the one. He wanted her in his life. He wanted to have a family with her. But, she'd made it pretty clear, they were over. There was nothing there. As he turned and made his way across the yard, he shoved his fists into his pockets. What a crappy Christmas.

CHAPTER TWENTY-FOUR

HANNAH

The next morning, Hannah laid in bed, staring up at the ceiling. The numbers on her clock shone brightly in her room. Six thirty. She needed to get up soon and get ready.

But, she was trying to forget the conversation she'd had with Logan last night. She tapped her fist on her forehead. Only problem was, it seemed that no amount of pushing it from her mind helped. His voice and his gaze were as fresh in her mind as if he was standing right next to her.

Groaning, she pulled her pillow over her face. She'd stay here for the rest of her life if she could.

A soft knock filled the silent room.

"Come in," she said, pulling the pillow off and tossing it on the floor.

"Hey, just wanted to let you know that you have about half hour before we need to get moving," her mom said, slipping into the room.

Hannah sat up. "Thanks, Mom."

"How'd it go last night?" Her mom's eyes sparkled as she nodded in the direction of the Blake's house.

Ugh. Her mom thought she was going to confess her feelings to Logan. "Fine. I told him I was marrying Samson."

"What?" Her mom stared at her.

"Mom, I'm marrying Samson." A sick feeling settled in her stomach. She hated lying to her. Not when they were trying to mend their relationship. "Oh, and I'm leaving right after the wedding."

Her mom's expression fell. Hannah hated hurting her like this.

"You're leaving? Again?"

"It's what's best." She pulled the covers from her body and swung her legs over the bed. The room felt as if it was closing in on her. She needed to do something.

"But, Christmas Eve is my holiday." Her mom's voice was weak as her gaze turned stony.

"Well, I'm marrying Samson and I have to consider his feelings as well. His mom wants us to come to a holiday party for their company. I have to go." Hannah stood and made her way over to the bathroom. "Thanks for understanding," she said as she shut the door on her mom's hurt expression.

Flipping on the water, Hannah climbed into the shower and cried. Cried for her love for Logan. Cried for how badly she had to treat her mom. And cried for Piper.

When she got out, she had no more tears. Splashing cold water on her face, she stared at herself. She needed to get a grip. This was her choice. All she needed to do was get through this wedding and then she'd get on a plane and fly away. Away from all of this pain.

She did her make-up and hair. As she walked into her room, she grabbed her phone. She'd missed a dozen texts from

Sandy. Hannah slipped on her shoes and opened her door. In the kitchen, she almost ran into Samson.

"Hey, Han. Sleep good?" he asked as he spooned some cereal into his mouth.

Hannah just nodded. "I've decided to leave today. After the wedding, we'll fly out to your parents' party."

Samson's eyes widened. "Seriously?"

Hannah pinched her lips together. "Yep."

"Awesome."

Hannah's mom walked in. She was dressed in her hospital scrubs. "I have to go in. Dr. Robinson is sick and I need to cover for her."

Hannah felt awful. Her mom seemed so upset. But what could she do? She had to leave. "Okay, Mom. Will you be back in time?"

She shrugged. "It's a twelve-hour shift, so probably not." She grabbed her purse that was hanging on the wall and pulled out her keys.

Hannah made her way over and pulled her mom into a hug, who stiffened from the contact. It didn't matter. It was Christmas. She was going to hug her mom. "I'll see you real soon."

She just nodded. "Okay."

Hannah hugged her again. "I love you."

"You, too." Her mom pulled from the hug and stepped back. "Have a safe flight," she said as she opened the garage door and stepped out.

"Mom?"

"Hannah."

"Merry Christmas."

Her mom gave her one last look and then shut the door behind her. Hannah's shoulders slumped as she turned. She hated doing this to her. The hurt was written all over her mom's face. Hannah wanted a better relationship, but it seemed she was always disappointing her mom.

Then Hannah squared her shoulders. Once things calmed down, she'd make more of an effort. It was evident they could make a relationship work. It would just take time.

Turning to Samson, Hannah forced a smile. "Ready?"

He nodded. "Let's do this so we can get out of here."

Hannah grabbed her purse and headed toward the front door. Time to get this wedding over with.

LOGAN

Music blared from the speakers as he walked into the reception hall. The wedding had been pleasant. Except for the fact that he had to see Hannah. She refused to link arms with him, so they walked down the aisle next to each other. And she refused to look at him during the ceremony.

And forget about talking. Every time he tried to approach her, she'd veer off to the side and engage in a conversation with someone he was sure she didn't know.

The reception hall had been decorated in a Christmas theme. Trees lined the walls and twinkled with lights. A buffet was set up on the far wall. Glancing around at the guests, Logan finally located Hannah. She was talking to Sandy.

This was his moment. She hadn't noticed him approach.

"You really have to go?" Sandy asked.

Hannah nodded. "Samson needs to get back."

Logan tried to keep his fists from clenching at the mention of that tool.

"Well, thanks for coming. And thanks for stepping in." Sandy reached out and hugged Hannah.

Hannah returned the hug. Then her gaze fell on him. "I should go," she said as she pulled away.

Sandy nodded, then turned her attention to an overzealous aunt, who pulled her away. Hannah glanced at him one more time and started to walk away.

Logan wasn't going to let her go this easily. "Wait," he said, reaching out and grabbing her elbow.

"I need to go."

"No. You need to tell me what happened. This isn't you. Marrying that guy? Come on." She needed to start talking.

"Please. It's what's best."

"What's best? For who?"

She chewed her lip as she glanced around. "For everyone."

What did that mean? "What happened to telling each other the truth? What's the truth, Hannah?"

She studied him, then shook her hand. "This is the truth."

Anger filled his chest. This wasn't the truth. He knew it, and she knew it.

"I gotta go. Our flight leaves at three." Hannah turned. Desperation raced up his spine. He needed her to stay.

"I bought that house."

She paused and turned. "What?"

"That house. The one in your family. I bought it."

Her eyes widened. "Why would you do that?"

He stared at her. Was she serious? How could she not know? "It was important to you. You wanted it back in your family."

"You—you bought it for me?"

He leaned in. "Maybe."

She shook her head. "You shouldn't have. We aren't together. That's something you do for your wife. For Charity." She nodded toward Charity, who was laughing and talking with a groomsman.

Logan turned his attention back to Hannah. "I don't want to be with her. I want—"

"Logan, I need to go." She turned, then glanced back at him. "Merry Christmas."

He opened his mouth to say something, but couldn't find the words. He wanted her to stay. Needed her to stay. Why wouldn't his mind form the words to tell her?

As much as his heart pounded, he stayed rooted in his spot. He was tired of trying to tell her that he cared. She always seemed to have an excuse as to why she couldn't return the sentiment. Maybe it was best to move on.

He turned so he didn't have to watch her disappear out the door. Or to watch her leave with Samson.

"Daddy?"

Forcing a smile, Logan glanced down at Piper, who was wearing a blush pink dress. She was staring up at him. Her red hair had been tamed into curls.

She smiled. "What's wrong? Where's Miss Hannah going?"

Logan cleared his throat. "She has to go home."

"She's not going to stay for Christmas?"

Logan shook his head. "Sorry, Pip. She probably won't be back for a long time."

Piper's face fell. "What? Why? Was it something I did?"

Logan grabbed her and lifted her up. "Nope. You did nothing. She's marrying that guy. That's the end of it."

Piper squealed, then her face grew serious as she placed both hands on his cheeks. "But you love her."

He stared at her. "What?"

"You love her, right? Like the prince loves Cinderella."

He set her down, then crouched low to meet her gaze. "Where did you hear that?"

Piper brushed down the front of her dress. "I heard Grandma tell Pops. Do you want to dance with her?"

He studied her. "Yes."

Her eyes were so big as she stared at him. "Then you love her." She seemed so matter-of-fact.

"But, it's... complicated."

"Does she know you want to dance with her?"

Logan shook his head.

"You should tell her."

"I should?"

Piper nodded. "When you dance, then you'll be married. And, if you get married, I can have her dolls."

Logan laughed. "Would you like that?"

Piper pinched her lips and nodded. "Yes. I like Miss Hannah."

His heart raced. Maybe Piper was right. He needed to tell Hannah. She had to know. He'd already let her walk out of his life without knowing the whole truth. He wasn't going to make that mistake again.

"Ma," he said, racing up to his mom, who was in the buffet line. "Watch Pip for me?"

His mom studied him, then nodded. "Sure."

"Thanks!"

He made his way to the door. Once outside, he rushed over to his truck. His heart pounded so hard, he thought it might burst from his chest.

"Hey." A hand wrapped around his arm and gave him a sharp tug.

Turning, he glanced down to see Charity staring up at him with fire in her gaze. "Not now."

"Where are you going?"

He stuck his key into his truck door and unlocked it. "We're done."

Her eyes widened. "What?"

"We're done. You and me. We've been done a long time ago. If you think I'm going to let you into my life just so you can disappoint our daughter on a daily basis, you're kidding yourself."

Her eyes widened as she stared at him. "What did that witch tell you?"

Logan stopped and turned around. "Excuse me?"

Charity's lips fluttered as she glanced around. "Hannah. What did she say to you?"

Slamming his door, he stepped toward her. "What's there to tell me?"

Charity took a step back. "Nothing."

"Charity?"

"Nothing, all right? Just some drunken things I may have said last night."

Logan narrowed his eyes. "About me?"

Charity stared at him. "She didn't tell you?"

He shook his head. "No. But you're going to."

She laughed and stepped toward him. "It was nothing."

"She threatened Hannah," a deep voice boomed from behind Logan. Turning, he saw the cab driver that was always driving Hannah around.

"You know?"

The man nodded as he walked up. "I heard the whole thing. This woman here threatened Hannah. Told her if she didn't back away, she was going to make your life a living hell. She would drag you to court for custody of your daughter."

"You were there when this happened?"

"Yep. I was there. I tried to convince Hannah not to go along with it, but she wouldn't listen. I couldn't sleep last night. It took me all day to find where this wedding was. I had to tell you."

Logan glanced back to Charity. "Why? Why would you do that to Piper? She loves you, and you treat her like garbage."

Then realization settled in his stomach. He knew why. "You want my money."

Charity laughed, a high-pitched laugh. Logan clenched his jaw. He should have known.

"That's why you came back. It had nothing to do with Piper or Christmas. You want my dad's money."

Charity stared at him. He could see the excuse she was trying to come up with race through her gaze. But then she shrugged. "So what? I'm sure there's a way to prove that you knew about that money before the divorce. You should have listed it as an asset."

Rage filled his stomach. "It was my dad's. I didn't even know he existed before we divorced. How would I have known?"

Charity's gaze flitted around. "Well, I'm still Piper's mom. That should get me a portion of the dough."

Logan stepped forward and lowered his voice. "If you threaten to use our daughter for your gain, I will bury you in court costs. And believe me, I have more money than you." He steeled his frustration and let his breath out slowly. "But that's not what Piper wants. So, here's what I'm going to do. I'm gonna forget that we had this conversation and go find Hannah. You are going to stay, because Piper wants you here for Christmas. But once the holidays are over, you are going to go back to whatever hole you crawled out of. If you agree to come visit her on holidays, I may consider giving you a stipend."

Charity's eyes widened, and her lips parted. Logan held up his finger.

"It will only come if you are the doting mom. If you—even once—fail our daughter again, you will lose everything." He lowered his gaze. "Do you understand me?"

Charity's face reddened as she pinched her lips. Finally, she let out a breath and nodded. "Deal."

A sick feeling settled in Logan's stomach. He hated the idea that he had to pay his ex to visit their daughter. But, he couldn't stand to see her so sad when Charity failed her. His dad gave him money to make him happy and, seeing his daughter happy made him happy. He was sure his dad would be okay with it.

"Now, go take care of our daughter," he said, nodding toward the reception hall.

Charity huffed, then headed back into the building.

Logan glanced over at the cab driver. "Thanks for doing that."

The man nodded and stuck out his hand. "Name's Bert. You're the neighbor boy?"

Logan met his gesture and nodded. "Logan."

"Nice to meet you."

They stood in silence for a moment. "I'm going to go get Hannah."

Bert stepped away from the truck. "You go do that. I never liked that fiancé of hers."

Logan slid into the cab. "Me, neither." He gave Bert a quick smile and slammed the door shut. He waited until Bert walked over to his cab, got in, and drove away.

Sticking the key into the ignition, Logan turned it. His truck sputtered a few times, then died. He gripped the steering wheel. Not now. Turning the key, he tried again. Same result. Slamming his hand down on the wheel, he glanced around. What was he going to do now?

CHAPTER TWENTY-FIVE

LOGAN

Logan cursed and swung open his door. Stepping out, he slammed the door and rushed back inside. The band had started up and half the room was up and doing the bunny hop.

Logan weaved in and out of the dancers until he found his mom and Piper. They were sitting at the table and had matching disgruntled looks.

"Hey, Mom. Where's Charity?"

His mom waved toward the buffet line.

"Daddy!" Piper hopped up from her seat and wrapped her arms around Logan's waist. "Can you tell Grandma that I don't eat Brussels sprouts?"

"What?" he asked, glancing down at the green vegetables on her plate. He sighed. "You can eat them, bug."

Piper folded her arms. "No. I don't eat those."

He turned to his mom. "I need a ride home. My truck isn't starting, and I need to get there before Hannah leaves."

His mom's eyes widened. "Why do you need to catch Hannah?"

His heart sped up from the question. "I'm going to tell her that I love her."

"He wants to dance with her," Piper added as she stepped to the side and twirled.

His mom gave him a smile. "It's about time," she said as she dug through her purse and emerged with a set of car keys.

"Great. Thanks." He grabbed the keys and started back toward the door.

"Daddy, wait!" Piper yelled. Logan stopped and turned to see his daughter sprint up to him. "I wanna come."

He picked her up and peered into her gaze. He gave her a serious look. "You can come only if you promise to help me convince Miss Hannah to dance with me."

She met his look. "Promise."

Grinning, he held onto her as he pushed through the door and out to the parking lot. It felt like an eternity before he found his mom's minivan and opened the door. Piper piled in and shut the door as he got into the driver's seat.

"Ready, Pip?"

"Let's go get Hannah!" she squealed as he started the car and pulled out of the parking lot.

The twenty-minute drive back to his house felt like it would never end. His heart pounded as he thought about the things he was going to say to her. He wasn't even going to allow her to talk. He was just going to lay it all out and hope she'd accept him. What did he have to lose?

His stomach sank as he pulled into her driveway and there were no lights on in the house. He shut off the car and pulled on the handle. Piper was already out of her seat and opening her door.

He steeled his nerves as he stepped up onto the walkway.

"I'll be right back, Daddy. I need to go pee," Piper said as she sprinted across the lawn and over to their house.

"Keys, Pip."

She raced back and grabbed them from him. "Thanks," she squealed and disappeared behind the house.

Logan glanced back to Hannah's house. He took a deep breath and walked up to the front door. To the massive wreath Miss Kathy had picked out. Reaching out, he knocked on the door. The sound was muffled by the green foliage.

After a second of waiting, he reached out and did it again. Nothing.

"Hannah?" he called out and then felt instantly stupid. If she wasn't going to answer his knocks, she probably wouldn't answer his calls.

"Daddy? Look," Piper said from behind him.

Turning, he saw Piper holding up the two American Girl doll boxes. His heart soared and sank at the same time.

"Why would Miss Hannah leave her dolls on our doorstep?" She stared up at him.

He grabbed the top box and a white slip of paper floated to the ground. He reached down and scooped it up. Unfolding it, he read it.

Dear Miss Piper,

These are for you. Merry Christmas. I know you will love them and take care of them. Play with them with your Mom. That's a relationship you will treasure.

Thank you for being such a sweet girl and letting me into your life. I will love you forever.

Love, Miss Hannah

He swallowed against the emotions that had risen in his throat.

"Miss Hannah's gone?"

Logan nodded. "We're too late."

A tear rolled down Piper's cheek. "Why would she go? She's your princess."

Logan reached out and wrapped his arms around Piper's shoulders. "It's okay. We'll see her again."

Piper sobbed into his shoulder. "But..." she started, but the rest got muffled by his shirt.

The sound of a car pulling into the driveway drew his attention up. Miss Kathy was staring at them through her windshield. Logan looked down and wiped Piper's tears.

"Why the long faces?" she asked as she shut the door behind her.

"Miss Hannah's gone," Piper sobbed.

Miss Kathy looked over at Logan. "She left already?"

Logan nodded. "We were hoping to catch her, but it looks like we were too late."

"Daddy was supposed to dance with her," Piper said.

Miss Kathy raised her eyebrows.

"I was going to ask her to stay." He felt a little strange confessing his feelings to her mom. "For us," he said as he wrapped his arm around Piper's shoulders.

Miss Kathy glanced around. "Well, let's go get her."

"What?" Logan asked.

"I made the mistake of walking away. While I was at work, I realized that I was done running away. If my daughter wants to spend Christmas in New York, then that's where I am going to be. If I want a better relationship, it starts with me."

Logan stood. "You want to go to New York?"

Miss Kathy nodded. "Let's do it."

Logan grabbed out his keys. "Grab the dolls, Piper. We're going to get Miss Hannah."

Piper looked confused, but grabbed the boxes. "Yay!"

He smiled at her. "That's how I feel. Yay!"

After an hour-long drive, Logan pulled his mom's van up

into the parking garage of the Wilmington airport. Piper jumped out, followed by Miss Kathy. They walked into the ticketing area, and Piper's eyes widened.

Logan lifted his hand as Miss Kathy started rifling around in her purse. "I've got this."

She smiled. "Thanks, Logan. Come on, Piper, let's go play with those dolls." She waved Piper over to the nearby benches.

Logan stepped up to the counter and an attendant smiled at him. "Merry Christmas," she said.

He nodded. "I need three tickets to New York. Preferably nonstop."

The attendant turned her attention to the monitor in front of her as she typed. Then she clicked her tongue. "I have a flight leaving in thirty minutes—"

"We'll take it." He pulled out his wallet.

"But there's a layover in Atlanta."

Logan lowered his card. "Really?"

She shrugged. "It's the only one we have three tickets for."

Glancing behind him, he saw Piper and Miss Kathy smiling and holding the dolls. He turned back around. "We'll make it work."

She took his card. "Perfect."

HANNAH

"Ladies and gentlemen, thank you for flying Delta this Christmas Eve. We hope your flight was enjoyable and have a happy holiday," the pilot's textured voice said over the intercom.

Hannah turned to Samson, who had pulled out his luggage and had it resting on his lap. His phone was already out, and he was busy typing. "My mom wants to know your dress size."

She stared at him. "She does? Why?"

Samson glanced over at her. "You can't wear that to my parents' dinner party. Now, what is it?"

Hannah chewed her lip. "Six."

He nodded as he typed. "Done." Slipping his phone into his pocket, he glanced around. "Why aren't we moving?"

A mom and dad were at the front, trying to wrestle their little boy out of the seat. He was shrieking and kicking. They were in the aisle, holding up all the passengers who wanted to get off.

All Hannah could do was smile. She felt bad for them. Especially since most of the people in line were shooting them dirty looks.

"Who takes kids on a plane?" Samson muttered. A few passengers who were standing next to their seat nodded in agreement.

"I don't think that they are trying to inconvenience us. They look pretty upset." Hannah nodded to their red faces and pinched lips.

"They should have known better."

"They need our compassion." Hannah glared at him. How could he be so judgmental? Her eyes widened. What had she gotten herself into? He was never going to change his mind. He didn't want kids and never would. She was fool to think things could be different.

"What?" he asked.

"Why are we doing this?"

"Doing what?"

"Why are we faking that we want a relationship?"

Samson stared at her. "You don't want to marry me?"

She swallowed. "Do you want to marry me?"

He glanced at her, then over to the toddler that they'd finally dislodged from the seat and were dragging from the plane. There was a collective sigh as the line started moving again. "No. Not if having kids is involved. I love what we have, but that's it. I don't want it to change."

The weight that Hannah had been carrying around these last few days lifted from her shoulders. Reaching over, she pulled the ring from her finger. "Here."

Samson studied her, then took it. "You sure?"

"I want kids."

He wrinkled his nose as he slipped the ring into his pocket. "Then I guess we're done."

Hannah sighed and gave him a small smile. "I guess we are."

The line dwindled down so Hannah stood and grabbed her carry-on from up above. Samson followed after her. As they walked down the walkway toward the airport, Samson glanced back to her.

"What's your plan?"

Hannah stepped out and glanced around. Families rushed around her, desperate to get to their plane that was most likely taking them home. "I'm going to go home."

"Back to North Carolina?"

She nodded. "Yeah. I'm going to spend Christmas with my mom."

Samson shouldered his briefcase and wrapped his hand around the handle of his luggage. "Do you need any help?"

Hannah shook her head. "Nope. I've got this."

He stood there, as if he wanted to say something. Hannah just smiled. "It's okay. Go. Your family's waiting."

Reaching out, he wrapped one arm around her shoulders. "Have a nice life, Hannah Bell."

She patted his back. "Merry Christmas."

He raised two fingers to his forehead and flicked them away. "Aye, aye, ma'am." Then turned and walked away.

Hannah's heart hurt. It was hard saying goodbye. But for

the first time in a long time, she wasn't running away from her problems. She was facing them. The strength that gave her caused her to smile.

She glanced around. An attendant stood behind a counter and was typing furiously on the keyboard in front of her. Hannah approached.

"Excuse me?" she said as she set her carry-on next to her.

"I'm sorry your flight was canceled, but it's not my fault," the attendant's raspy voice said as she glanced up, her eyes wide.

Hannah stepped back. "I'm sorry. My flight isn't canceled. I actually need to buy one."

The attendant's gaze swept over Hannah. Her fingers stopped typing so she could take a drink from the mug next to her. "I apologize," she said and put the mug back down. "It's been kind of hectic around here." She gave Hannah a smile. "You need a flight?"

Hannah nodded. "Yes."

"Where to?"

"I need to get to North Carolina as soon as possible." Then Hannah gave her a smile. "I need to be with Mom." And Logan. But that ship had sailed. She needed to push him from her mind.

The attendant typed on the keyboard again. "I can get you to Wilmington, but there will be a layover in Atlanta. Will that work?"

Hannah chewed her nail, then sighed. "I guess."

The attendant's fingers flew again. Soon the printer whirred, and her tickets were spit out. The attendant put the tickets into an envelope and handed them to Hannah.

"Flight leaves in twenty minutes. Gate Forty."

Hannah nodded and took the tickets. Once she located the gate, she stood in line with the other waiting passengers. The realization of what had happened sunk in. Samson was gone, and she was alone.

She swallowed. And her mom was gone at work until tomorrow. Yet again, she was alone. Wrapping her arms around her chest, she sighed. It was a feeling she was getting used to.

CHAPTER TWENTY-SIX

LOGAN

Piper nearly bounded out of her seat as the plane pulled into the gate. Logan had made the mistake of getting her one of the holiday cookies the attendants were selling. Sugar, mixed with exhaustion, made a hyper Piper.

"We should grab some food," Logan said, leaning over to Miss Kathy.

She nodded. "Good idea."

They waited until the plane was empty, then got up themselves. As they walked down the walkway, Logan glanced down at his tickets. "We have about an hour until the next flight, so we should do this fast."

"Okay," Miss Kathy said.

Once they were in the airport, Logan glanced around. When he saw a security guard, he approached him. "McDonalds?"

The guard waved his hand, motioning down the terminal. Logan thanked him and called for Piper to follow. They walked in the direction the guard had indicated until they found a McDonalds. Relieved, Logan left Piper with Miss Kathy and approached the counter.

He ordered and the teller gave him a receipt and told him to wait. He leaned against a nearby pillar and glanced around. Miss Kathy had some soothing effects on Piper. She was rubbing her back and talking to her. Piper had calmed and was resting her chin in her hand.

Someone bumped against his shoulder.

The woman kept her head down. "Excuse me," she said as she continued walking.

"No problem," he said, glancing over to her retreating frame. There was something familiar about the way her blonde hair cascaded down her shoulders. Thinking back, there was something familiar about the melodies of her voice.

He stared, almost too stunned to believe it. "Hannah?" he asked, but she was too far to hear him.

Racing after her, he fell into step with her. Her head was down as she stared at her phone. But, he'd know the curve of her lips and splash of freckles anywhere. Grabbing her arm, he pulled her from the crowd.

Instantly, her gaze shot up. Her lips were parted as if she was about to give him a piece of her mind. But she stopped. "Logan?"

Reaching out, he pulled her into a hug. Everything about holding her body next to him felt right. When he pulled back, he glanced down at her. "I thought you were in New York," he said.

She stared at him. "I thought you were in North Carolina." Then she glanced around. "Where's Charity?"

"She's back at the reception. Or at my house." He shoved his hands into his pockets. "I don't really know."

A groan escaped her lips. "What? You shouldn't be here."

Logan straightened. "I know."

She narrowed her eyes. "Know what?"

"What Charity threatened you with." He reached out and touched her shoulder. "I told her she was kidding herself if she thought I was going to let that fly. All she wanted me for was my money. I won't have that. Not when I love someone else."

Hannah's eyes widened, but then she furrowed her brow. "But what about Piper? I won't let her drag that little girl through the mud. I love her too much."

Logan thought his heart would burst from her words. She loved his daughter. That meant everything to him. "Don't worry, I'll keep Piper safe. Charity's reach will only go so far." He paused as he watched her mull his words around in her mind.

"I love you." There. He said it.

Her gaze snap back up to him. "What?"

"I love you. It's as simple as that. I know I've complicated things in the past. I know I've hurt you. But, Hannah"—his voice grew deep as emotions filled his throat—"I love you. Truly and completely. There is no one else in the world I want to be with than you." He smiled over to her. "I want to have a family with you."

Her eyes widened as her lips parted. Her beautiful, pink lips. "I—"

He reached out and pulled her close. "Don't think. Do you love me, too?"

She glanced around as if unable to meet his gaze. "I don't want to hurt Piper like that."

He leaned down and captured her gaze with his own. "I have a feeling Piper won't mind. She already loves you more than me." Then he leaned forward until his lips brushed her ear. "Besides, I think you've won over her heart since you gave her those dolls."

She pulled back and looked at him "You found those?"

He nodded, then grew serious. "Please say you forgive me."

Her face stilled. "For what?"

"For hurting you all those years ago. I was a stupid boy. I didn't know what I was doing."

Tears formed on Hannah's lids. She stared at him. "Of course," she whispered. "I forgive you."

He smiled at her. "That was easy."

She reached out and swatted his shoulder. "Hey, now."

He feigned hurt for a moment before he pulled her close again. "Let's do it again. Say you love me."

She studied him, then shook her head. "No."

His stomach sank. "What?"

She chewed her bottom lip. "I'm tired of talking." Suddenly, she pressed her lips against his and everything around him faded away.

Wrapping his arms around her waist, he pulled her to him. Everything about her. The way her lips felt. The way her body fit against his. The way the smell of her hair filled his every sense. All of it was familiar. All of it said home.

Her lips moved against his as he deepened the kiss. Her fingers weaved their way into his hair. He never wanted to let her go.

He groaned when she pulled away. "Why'd you do that?" he asked.

Her lips were puffy as she glanced up at him. "I love you, Logan Blake," she said.

Pulling her close, he softly pressed his lips against hers. "I know," he whispered.

She swatted him again.

He reached down and kissed a trail from her nose to her ear. "But you're going to have to stop hitting me," he whispered.

She giggled. "I will when you stop saying ridiculous things."

"Did she say she'll dance with you?" Piper's voice asked from behind them.

Hannah snapped away from him. "Piper?" She glanced over to her mom. "Mom?"

Logan smiled. "Oh, I forgot to tell you that they came with me."

Crouching down, she pulled Piper into a hug. "I thought you had to work, Mom."

Miss Kathy's face grew serious. "It's Christmas. It's time for family. It's time for moving on. I wasn't going to let my little girl leave again. If you were only going to be happy in New York with Samson, then I was going, too."

Logan could see the tear slip down her face as she let go of Piper and stood. "I'm so sorry, Mom."

Miss Kathy shook her head and extended her arms. "All is forgiven if you can forgive me, too."

Hannah nodded and rushed to her mom's arms. They embraced. Logan couldn't help but feel complete.

"So, did she dance with you?" Piper asked again.

Reaching down, Logan hoisted her up into his arms. "What do you think, Pip?"

She studied him. "You look too happy. So, I'm going to guess... yes?"

Logan wrapped her into a hug and kissed her cheek. "Yep. She's here to stay."

She gripped her dolls in her arms. "Good."

Logan wrapped his free arm around Hannah and Miss Kathy walked beside her as they made their way down the terminal.

He heard Hannah giggle. "What?" he asked, glancing down.

She smiled up at him. "Bert was right. Christmas is a magical time."

His heart surged at the words. She was right. Reaching down, he brushed his lips against hers. All he'd ever wanted for Christmas was right here, wrapped in his arms.

EPILOGUE

Hannah sat on the roof of the deck, surrounded by tulle. She had slipped out here to catch a breather from Sandy. Man, when that girl wasn't the one getting married, she was a slave driver. It didn't help that her opinion clashed with Hannah's mother's. They were like two Rottweilers fighting over the last bone.

Brushing down her wedding dress, Hannah glanced out to where the sun gleamed off the ocean. She was getting married today. She couldn't believe it. She looked down at her ring and her heart soared. Logan and Piper had done such a good job picking it out.

"Fancy meeting you out here, beautiful."

Logan's voice sent shivers down her back. Turning, she smiled, then realization hit her. He wasn't supposed to see her in her dress.

"Logan!" She gathered the skirt toward herself. "You're not supposed to see me."

His eyes widened as the dress got pulled up to her thigh.

"Miss Hannah, I do declare," he said, wiggling his eyebrows.

She shot him a look, and he just grinned back at her.

"Tonight, my dear. Save it for tonight," he said, his voice husky.

Her cheeks heated as she smiled at him. Butterflies erupted in her stomach. Forcing a serious face, she waved toward his tux. "Why are you out here?"

Logan leaned back on his hands. "Had to take a break. Man, when Jimmy's not getting married, he's a task master."

Hannah giggled. "I know, right? I thought pregnancy would slow Sandy down"—Hannah shook her head—"It's only made her meaner. And more organized."

Logan laughed. Hannah felt the stress of the morning leave her body. Even with the craziness of everything around her, she was making the best choice today. She couldn't wait to marry Logan.

His face stilled as he studied her. "I love you, Hanny B."

She smiled over to him. "I love you, too."

He crawled across the roof until he was at the edge. "Marry me?"

She would have scooted down to meet him, but was too afraid of snagging her dress on the shingles. "You already asked me."

He nodded. "I just want to hear you say it again."

She rolled her eyes. "Yes. I will marry you, Logan Blake."

Leaning back, he smiled at her. "I've still got it."

"Hannah Bell, what in the world are you doing out here on the roof?" Sandy's voice carried from inside her room. Sheepishly, she glanced over to Logan.

"I gotta go."

Logan glanced back to his window. "Yeah. I'd hate for them to find me missing."

Hannah stood and gathered her skirt into her arms. "See you on the other side?"

Logan blew her a kiss. "Of course, babe. Soon, everyone will be gone and it will be just me and you—"

"And me!" Piper called from inside Hannah's room. All the girls were getting ready at her house. The guys were getting ready at Logan's.

"And Piper," Logan added. "At our house." Then he leaned in. "But not tonight. Tonight, it will be just you and me..." His gaze turned serious as he smiled at her.

"Can't wait," Hannah said as excitement flitted through her body. Sandy tsked her as she handed the skirt to waiting hands.

"I'll be the one at the end of the aisle," Logan called.

"Can't wait!" Hannah repeated as she slipped into her room and shut the door. A smile played on her lips. This was all she'd ever wanted and it was happening. Piper rushed over to her and gave her a hug.

Hannah's mom appeared in the doorway. "Ready, Hannah?"

Patting Piper on the head, she glanced up. "Yep. Let's get going."

Her mom and Sandy helped hold her dress so she could descend down the stairs without tripping. At the bottom, she glanced around. Bert stood next to the door with a suit on. Hannah smiled. "You look good."

Bert grinned and rubbed his bald head. "Yeah, I can clean up nice if I want." He opened the door and waved toward his cab with the words *Bert's Cab Service* written across the side. Logan had decided to put his money to good use and invested in Bert's taxi company. He'd been able to buy five cars with the money and was already talking about retiring.

"Your chariot awaits," he said, extending his hand.

Hannah glanced over to him and smiled. Reaching out, she

gave him a big hug. "Thanks for everything you've done for me."

Bert patted her back. "You bet," he said, his voice gruff.

Hannah pulled back. "Are you crying?"

Bert wiped at his eyes. "What? No. Allergies."

Hannah raised an eyebrow. "Right."

"Wedding won't wait; hop to it, m'lady."

"I'm the bride," Hannah said as she made her way out the front door.

"Well, then, everyone's waiting for you," he said, following after her.

Hannah paused on the stoop and glanced around. Logan was walking down the sidewalk toward one of cabs that lined the street. He turned and winked at Hannah. She smiled. Her heart felt as if it would burst. Her mom came up next to her and wrapped an arm around her.

"Ready to go, sweetie?"

Hannah nodded. "Let's do this."

***

Want more Anne-Marie Meyer romances? Head on over and grab you next read HERE.

For a full reading order of Anne-Marie's books, you can find them HERE.

Made in the USA
Monee, IL
07 January 2024